Pipe Dreams

by

Ashantay Peters

Pipe Dreams

Cover Art by *Diana Carlile*

The Wild Rose Press, Inc.
PO Box 708
Adams Basin, NY 14410-0708
Visit us at www.thewildrosepress.com

Publishing History
First Fantasy Edition, 2015
Print ISBN 978-1-62830-836-5
Digital ISBN 978-1-62830-837-2

Published in the United States of America

"So are you the new owner of this wreck?"

Her hands clenched, along with her jaw. "I'm the proud owner of what will soon be a lovely home."

He snorted. "You planning to have this in shape any time before winter? Because from where I'm standing, you'll need more than a mop."

Abigail's ears heard echoes of Rich. "I have power tools, and I know how to use them. You have an issue with that?"

"No, I don't have an issue. You've got work ahead of you. Just sayin'. I guess you'll be hiring a crew for the big stuff, right?"

Abigail threw her shoulders back. This guy sounded exactly like Rich. Bossy. "I can handle it." She'd already sub-contracted the larger jobs, but that wasn't his business.

His mouth drew into a tight line, his hands fisted on his hips. "Sorry to bother you. I stopped because it looked like you might need a hand. Guess I misunderstood."

Dropping his hands, Carlos turned to leave, looking back with a frown. "Good luck with this place. Come on, Henry, we're not needed here."

Henry paused, allowing her to ruffle his fur. He broke into a run, following the pissed-off man. An imp on her shoulder prodded her to call after him, "Bye, Henry. You can come visit anytime." Sotto voce she added, "But leave your human home."

The dog's owner kept walking with his shoulders up around his chin.

"Men," she huffed under her breath. "Just a bunch of know-it-all jackasses. And the good-looking ones are the worst."

Chapter One

The old man lay dying. His imminent passing punctuated every strangled breath. He figured that Lydia awaiting him was his undeserved reward for a lifetime of mistakes. She'd made one final request he needed to fulfill before he rejoined her. It was past time to handle the matter.

Where had Lydia said she'd put those letters he'd promised to forward? If only he hadn't waited. Now he didn't have the strength to leave his bed.

"Nurse! Nurse!"

What delayed her? Didn't she realize he needed her *now*?

Gathering himself to call again, he exhaled. He sensed a tug at his chest, an odd pulling sensation.

The old man viewed his frail body lying on the bed. He pinched his arm with two fingers but didn't feel the tweak. Hospital bed, dresser, chair, window, the room appeared different from usual.

He slowly understood that his view came from a distance, and his perspective originated above the room rather than from his bed. As if he floated at the ceiling. Because that's where his consciousness hovered, near the light fixture, until he moved further away. He raised his arm to brace himself against the ceiling, but his hand continued through into the attic.

What the heck? Lydia had told him this would

happen. She'd said he'd separate from his body at death. He drifted higher. No! He couldn't leave life yet. Not until he kept his promise to her.

The caretaker returned to the room. She searched for a pulse then gently replaced his hand and closed his eyelids. Lifting the sheet, she pulled it toward his head.

Panic flooded him. She should be trying to resuscitate him, not cover his body.

Then he noticed a shimmering golden cord linking him to his body. The cord. Maybe he wasn't too late to get back. He tugged. The golden light disintegrated.

Action, he needed to act. Frantic swimming motions landed him beside the bed. The old man pushed against his empty husk of a body, but his hand passed through. He shouted at the nurse. Couldn't she see him beside her? Waving his hands, he pushed at her arm. Why didn't she help him? See, hear, or feel him? He couldn't die. He wasn't ready.

She left the room and he followed. His last hope of regaining consciousness ceased along with his body functions. He had to be dead because he hadn't moved so fast in decades.

But, wait. Where was Lydia? She'd promised to meet him when he passed. Something was wrong. Very wrong.

****

Eighteen Months Later

"I've been waiting for you."

The barely heard whisper caught her attention. Abigail Stephens stopped in mid-motion and drew her hand back from her new home's doorknob. She looked to both sides and behind her at an empty yard.

Shrugging, she unlocked the door and grasped the

knob. Her fingers met cold metal, too icy for an early summer day in Blue Peak, North Carolina.

"'Bout time you got here. I need help."

The indistinct words sounded like a dry rustle, a pretense of words. Abigail hoped a neighbor's kid was teasing her. The alternative? Talking with dead people? Please, not again.

She backed off the porch, glancing at the overgrown shrubs. Dry branches, thrust up in bare, spiny fingers, revealed the house's foundation. No one hid there. The neglected Cape Cod before her made the Munsters' home look like a prime piece of real estate.

Abigail marched up the stairs, grabbed hold, twisted, and watched the knob come off in her hand. Throwing it down, she set her shoulder against the door and pushed. Dry hinges squealed as she moved into the small foyer.

"Holy crap. This place sounds like a haunted house. What was I thinking?"

After years of renovating homes, she believed each structure had a personality, a spirit that her work released. Her ex-husband, Rich, hadn't agreed, but that had been just one idea of many they hadn't seen eye-to-eye on. She shook her head to rid his image from her mind. Her new home wasn't haunted, just ignored.

A blast of cold, musty air blew past her like an escaped exhalation. Chill bumps rose on her neck. Looking around the interior, she doubted her initial to-do list even began to cover the work needed.

"I may have bitten off too much."

Rich's voice sounded in her mind. "You've done it this time. I'll try to pull us out with a profit, but I damn sure don't see how it'll happen."

Abigail's indignant huff filled the room. The jerk's memory wasn't worth her brain cells, but his image haunted her. Rich had never understood her dreams of owning a home and of making money with her art. He rarely saw past the surface. That's probably why he'd dumped her and married that young—

She shook her head, banishing the memories while knowing they'd return. Now she needed to move fast to make this place livable. Starting with pulling down those dusty velvet drapes.

Loud music shattered the neighborhood's quiet, cutting through her worries. She ran to the porch. "What in the world?"

Strains of the Beatles' "Magical Mystery Tour" blasted her, the sound waves flying past almost before she recognized the song. A candy apple red, vintage Mustang convertible in cherry condition rolled into view. Envy grabbed her breath, holding it hostage.

The car pulled in next door. As its engine shut down, quiet plummeted over the street. Perhaps her house had sat empty for a reason other than its dilapidated state.

An older woman who could have bought the car new off the showroom floor swung her legs out of the low-slung car. Her purple caftan caught on the doorframe when she reached in to the convertible's back seat. Riotous curls fell forward as she lifted out several bags, and her multitude of bracelets glittered in the sun.

Just her luck a loud hippie lived next door. And she owned Abigail's dream car.

Squinting at the hippie's stop sign hair color, she checked her own appearance. Her dust-coated, scuffed work boots, faded bib overalls, and worn leather gloves weren't "meet the neighbor" garb. A groan worked its way up her chest. Of course someone would show *after* she'd changed from her tailored slacks and silk blouse.

Walking around the car, the woman called out, "Hey, welcome neighbor!"

Crap. Too late to duck back into the house.

The woman moved closer, sun sparkling off her hair formed a halo effect. Abigail had always wanted red hair, or any color other than the dishwater blonde she cursed as her mother's inheritance. She pushed escaping strands of her fine, straight hair into her utilitarian ponytail. Great first impression coming right up. Or not.

Her neighbor swayed toward Abigail on platform shoes that looked original to the 1970s, her bangles and dangles creating accompanying music. A direct blue-eyed gaze examined Abigail.

"When did you move in?"

"I closed on the house early this morning. I'm Abigail Stephens." A quick appraising look revealed the woman had high cheekbones, a wide smile, firm chin, and flawless skin. Her hair color looked natural, but maybe she had a talented beautician. Abigail inhaled a light jasmine aroma. She'd expected patchouli.

The older woman waited at the bottom of Abigail's front stairs. "I hope you don't think I'm always blasting music, but I just love these first warm days of summer. I'm Sally Ford." She stepped up, and her hand met Abigail's in a firm shake. "It sure is great to know the stuck energy is getting cleared out of this place. It's not good to have a house sit empty."

Unsure how to respond, Abigail searched for a

comment. "My renovations are just starting. Will it bother you if I have a small dumpster here?"

"No problem. I'm glad the house will have a person," Sally tilted her head to the side, "or is it people?"

She shuffled her feet. "Just me."

Sally squinted, her lips puckered. "No animal friends? Romantic interest?"

"Just me," she repeated, her back stiffening. *Talk about nosy.*

Hands fisted on her hips Sally said, "Well, that'll change, soon. In fact, I know someone who will be perfect for you. Yep. I can almost see him in your aura.

"Oh, you have the drapes down already," Sally continued. Her neighbor's forefinger became an elegant pointer. "Great way to start out, and good feng shui, too. I bet the material held all kinds of stuff. Let me know if you need sage to smudge. I keep a supply handy. Never know when you'll need to clear out negative vibes."

"Thanks." What planet did her weirdo neighbor inhabit? Stuck energy? Smudge? Aura?

"Well, if you need anything, just let me know. I own Good Vibes downtown, and I'll be happy to help you out. See ya, hon!" Sally sashayed to her pale rose-colored house. "Don't forget to come see me," she called and disappeared through her front door.

Abigail shook like she'd been using power tools for too long. Good Vibes must be the place downtown, the store with the funky stuff out front. This morning she'd decided it'd be fun to check out when she had time. Now she feared going near the place.

Glancing at the convertible, she gathered the rest of

her cleaning supplies and walked inside. What had she let herself in for? Somehow she'd taken the turn to woo-woo land without noticing the curve.

****

The Collective Unconscious Café's door fell shut behind Carlos Young. He rolled his shoulders and walked toward Good Vibes. He didn't know why he had a gut feeling his mother wanted to speak with him in person. He'd long ago stopped wondering about or mentioning his instinctive reactions to her. She'd attribute his actions to some oddball metaphysical philosophy. His impulses could be explained with science. More likely by the extensive knowledge base he had about the parent he called by her first name in public. The woman who interfered with his love life as if Mom Knew Best.

He pushed into the store and saw his mother dancing to classic rock. "You look like a toddler with a new toy. Good lunch?"

Sally wriggled in place. "I met my new neighbor, Carlos. You're going to lov-um-like her. Very nice person, but a little quiet."

He silently poked through her candle display. Damn it. He should have called instead of walking over. Maybe he should get his mom antenna surgically removed. It'd potentially mean a frontal lobotomy, though the idea held promise at times.

"Yes, she's pretty with those blonde cheerleader-type looks, but reserved, uptight. You know, the type you like to rescue. Mid-thirties maybe. Wears frumpy work clothes and hmmm, I wonder why she hides her body."

Her caught her sidelong glimpse and repressed a

7

sigh.

"Did I tell you I saw a man and a small dog or large cat in her aura?"

"Mom, stop with the aura stuff. You know I don't believe the way you do." He laughed. "If I know you, she didn't get to say much. Hold on. A single woman bought the Wilkinson wreck?"

Sally emitted a game show buzzer sound. "Wrong. It's not a wreck. That house has tons of potential. She said she's started renovations but I saw no one else there. Could be rehabbing the place herself. You should stop and introduce yourself. She may need a hand."

Carlos leaned against the counter. "A hand? Or a band, as in wedding band? You don't fool me, Mom. Stop with the matchmaking." He pushed away from the counter and studied the card rack. "I know you want grandkids, but I'd like to do the choosing myself, okay?"

"But you're in each other's aura, um, never mind."

He plunked a bag of votive candles onto the counter. "Put these on my account, please. I need to get back to my real business." He enveloped her in a hug. "I love you, but you're a pain in my butt sometimes. I'm not ready to settle down just yet, but soon. I promise. I'll start looking around for your daughter-in-law. Maybe next year."

Carlos grabbed the candles and turned to leave.

"You don't have to ask her out. Just stop and say hello."

He glared at her. "Don't even start."

"That glare won't work. You learned it from me." Sally smirked. "Besides, introducing yourself is the neighborly thing to do."

He snorted. "Right. I live three blocks away."

"Yes, but I live right next door and you're my son, and you'll be seeing each other when you both come to dinner. I thought I taught you better manners than that."

"You're slipping on the guilt tripping, Mom." He sighed. "I'll stop by later."

"Great. And you can stay for dinner."

His gaze slid to the side. He hurried for the door. "Later this week, I meant." He stopped with his hand on the knob. "If she's taken on the Wilkinson house, she's got her hands full. Do everyone a favor and leave her be."

She squawked, "What do you mean?"

"You know what I mean." The door closed behind him.

Sally stuck her head out the door. "You can't avoid her, sweetie. She's your future."

Cripes. Next time he got a mom vibe he'd telephone. From Timbuktu.

****

Abigail rubbed her neck. She ached all over and her work had just begun.

An elusive whiff of tobacco smoke along with a muted sigh sounded in her ear. "I'm glad you're here."

"Hello? Is someone at the door?"

No one answered. She sniffed but couldn't find the odor's origin. Odd, the tobacco smelled fresh. How could that...must be her imagination.

Her skin crawled as a chill ran over her. She spoke aloud, hoping her voice would quiet her jitters. "The sun is going down. Quitting time."

Abigail packed and hurried out, the drive to her temporary apartment facing her tired body like a

9

Himalayan trek. A flash of light caught her eye as she drove away. Slamming on the brakes, she looked back at the house. She blinked and checked again.

No lights. How could there be? She hadn't planned to stay so late her first day. The electricity wouldn't get turned on until tomorrow.

Her truck fishtailed out of the drive in a steady acceleration.

Chapter Two

Though it was early June, mornings in the North Carolina mountains could be cool. The furnace had kicked in without hesitation, but the forced air hadn't yet warmed the house. Chills ran in waves over Abigail's body, and she reached for her extra sweatshirt.

Her shivers intensified when cool air swirled around her.

A quick look out the nearest window verified the trees were motionless. No breezes, no obvious drafts. Nada. Zip. No reasonable explanation for the cool, damp air sweeping past.

Nope, she didn't want to face the unthinkable. A ghost. She hadn't asked the realtor if the house had a haunted history. Abby hadn't noticed anything odd on her inspection or final walk-through. If she had, she'd have found another house. Not that many options existed in her price range, not in Blue Peak.

"Uh, uh. No way. I stopped believing in ghosts a long time ago."

"Are you sure about that?"

The low whispery sound had her heartbeat rattling her ribs. Eyes wide she swung around, hands frozen to the mop she held. The coolness kept pace, wrapping her in tentacles. Her breaths rasped, lungs heaved.

She'd never experienced the like. Not even when her dead grandparents had come to visit. But that had been her imagination. Her mother had told Abigail she didn't speak with dead people because ghosts don't exist. Spots danced in front of her eyes.

Wait, what was that dark shape? A shadow? Or—?

A low voice sounded in her ear. "If you aren't going to listen, get out. I need someone who'll help me."

Her ears rang. She screamed but made no sound. Holding the mop like a shield with sweating hands, she ran for the door.

****

Carlos scanned the coffee house he'd named The Collective Unconscious Café in a fit of whimsy. Blue Peak College's graduation ceremony this weekend boosted his business but reminded him of Sierra and the teaching profession he'd left.

Her defection still hurt at times. No, damn it, he wouldn't miss his ex-fiancée or the commitment he'd thought they'd made. She'd left him. Move on, already.

Too bad he'd wanted more than Sierra could give him. As he glanced over his customers' faces, mostly female, he saw plenty of hopeful smiles thrown his way. He needed to start dating, but God, he hated that scene.

Carlos turned to his young baristas. "All the food orders are out and Henry needs a break." *So do I.* "I'll be back in about fifteen minutes. Call if you need me."

His two employees nodded and turned aside. He didn't doubt they rolled their eyes at him. Sure, he should lighten up and let them handle more duties. He'd think about that next week.

He opened his office door and whistled. His Border collie, Henry, scrambled. "You ready to go buddy?"

Henry shook himself and ran to the leash lying on the desk, his body quivering.

"Let's take a ride. I need to clear out some cobwebs." Carlos often drove to talk out his concerns. Henry served as confessor, only because Sierra had hated his long-time friends. He'd lost track of his buddies long ago, many of who had left the area. Plus, he'd recently read a scientific study that proved dogs could interpret human speech. Worked for him.

They left through the separate office entrance and piled into an old, well-kept Volvo station wagon. Henry settled into the shotgun position, waiting for the window to lower. They drove off, Henry's black and white fur blown back by the motor-powered breeze.

Carlos drove aimlessly for a few minutes and decided to head back when his attention was attracted by an odd sight.

A blonde woman in overalls stood in the Wilkinson wreck's driveway, her back to the street. Her shoulders appeared tight with tension, but that could be because she held a mop straight out before her, almost like a shield. Her ponytail jittered, the only movement on a body that seemed frozen in place. Suddenly the mop jumped, as if her muscles had unlocked. This situation looked too strange not to stop.

****

Abigail raced into her yard, shivering. She looked over her shoulder hoping goblins hadn't followed her.

Her shoulders heaved with her efforts to breathe. Her muscles were locked, holding the mop in place before her. Sunshine warmed her neck, and she heard the sounds of lawnmowers and children playing. Normal sounds. Normal sensations. The house loomed behind her.

A cold and wet something shoved against her hand. "Eeeekkk!" Heart pounding in double time, she clutched her chest.

"Hey," a deep male voice said, "it's a dog nose, not slime."

A Border collie stood at her knee. She bent and ruffled his fur. "Hey, big guy. Sorry if I scared you." Giving his fur a last pat, she straightened and met a startled hazel gaze.

A man in his late thirties with wavy dark hair stared back. She noted several silvery locks fell casually onto his wide forehead. Dark framed glasses gave him a scholarly air. Her quick glance scanned a solid, six-feet tall swimmer's build—broad shoulders and narrow hips concealed with khaki slacks, a geometric patterned shirt, and track shoes. Nice, but she didn't have time for men.

His intense stare, highlighted by the glasses, got under her skin. What was biting The Professor's butt?

"We stopped to see if something's wrong. Are you all right?"

"Nothing's wrong." Oh, no wonder he'd been staring. "Really. Everything's fine."

He frowned. "It didn't look fine from where we were sitting. You held that mop like a distress flag."

"I'm fine. Thanks for stopping." Whew. Her blood pounded like, well, like it hadn't before. Maybe she needed a medical exam.

He wiped his right hand on his pant leg and held it out. "Carlos Young. I own Blue Peak's coffee house, the Collective Unconscious Café. I hope you'll stop by for a free welcome-to-town drink."

His hand surrounded hers. Warm. Nice. "I'm Abigail Stephens."

He patted the dog's head. "This is Henry."

She'd planned on heading for the café later today. Now she'd look like a user. Well, he *had* offered a drink. She cleared her throat and looked over his shoulder.

He shifted from foot to foot, his attention on the dog nosing in the tall grass. "So are you the new owner of this wreck?"

Her hands clenched, along with her jaw. "I'm the proud owner of what will soon be a lovely home."

He snorted. "You planning to have this in shape any time before winter? Because from where I'm standing, you'll need more than a mop."

Abigail's ears heard echoes of Rich. "I have power tools, and I know how to use them. You have an issue with that?"

"No, I don't have an issue. You've got work ahead of you. Just sayin'. I guess you'll be hiring a crew for the big stuff, right?"

Abigail threw her shoulders back. This guy sounded exactly like Rich. Bossy. "I can handle it." She'd already sub-contracted the larger jobs, but that wasn't his business.

His mouth drew into a tight line, his hands fisted on his hips. "Sorry to bother you. I stopped because it looked like you might need a hand. Guess I misunderstood."

Dropping his hands, Carlos turned to leave, looking back with a frown. "Good luck with this place. Come on, Henry, we're not needed here."

Henry paused, allowing her to ruffle his fur. He

broke into a run, following the pissed-off man. An imp on her shoulder prodded her to call after him, "Bye, Henry. You can come visit anytime." Sotto voce she added, "But leave your human home."

The dog's owner kept walking with his shoulders up around his chin.

"Men," she huffed under her breath. "Just a bunch of know-it-all jackasses. And the good-looking ones are the worst."

She tossed down the mop and grabbed a water bottle, gulping the liquid in one go. "Oh criminy. I must have seemed an idiot holding that mop, looking like I'd seen a gh—"

The unfinished thought fell under a rapid, crushing load of denial. He'd reminded her of Rich, intimating she lacked the necessary brains and skills for successful home renovation.

"I don't need another smart ass man giving me directions. Nuh, uh. Cripes, I've gotta stop talking to myself."

Her move to Blue Peak meant independence and more. Pipe, or real, they were her dreams, and this house counted as step one. She'd show him, she'd show them all. No interfering man or possible ghost would stop her success.

****

"Henry, that woman is a mess. Damn, but Mom's right. She is my type, but trouble. Not a doubt."

Carlos had planned to drive in the other direction when he'd left Collective Unconscious. Instead, he'd landed where his mom wanted him. He glanced at the dog. "I screwed up, didn't I?"

Henry responded with an open-mouthed dog grin,

his pink tongue lolled to the side. The wind blowing into the car disheveled his fur.

His first look at her had taken his breath away. Torn the air from his lungs.

Fine blonde hair with lighter highlights around her face. Her blue eyes had a slight almond shape at the corners. No make-up but a healthy facial color and full pink lips. Her bib overalls were loose, but not so baggy he didn't catch the way they fit over her rounded hips and breasts. She stood taller than average, but her gentle curves kept her from the scrawny appearance Sierra favored. Her hands were trim, slender, but without the pampered manicured look.

Her appearance hadn't stolen his oxygen so much as her expression. Frightened but determined. Resolute yet fragile might be the better description. He'd been a sucker for distressed females his whole life, seemed like. The woman faced more than overwhelming physical labor.

Carlos's fingers tapped the steering wheel. "She's got a temper. Maybe calling her new house a wreck hadn't been my best move."

The dog stared steadily at his human, his pants slow and soft.

"She probably thinks I'm an asshole. Sucks, that's what. My canine friend, the human world is perverse."

Henry stuck his head out the window.

He needed a woman, and not the one he'd just left. Dogs were man's best friend but weren't a substitute for hot sex. Getting laid while his mom hovered next door hoping for grandkids wasn't in his plans, though. He'd casually dated many of the females in town after Sierra left, but none kept his interest. Guess he'd give Jillian or Laura a try next.

****

Pleased with her progress, Abigail gathered and stored her tools. After Carlos left, the cool air and oppressiveness in the house had dissipated. Likely the odd sounds, smells, and cold were normal in a home shut up for over a year. She'd finally stopped looking over her shoulder.

Now crystals tinkled on the dining room chandelier. Abigail froze. She checked the trees outside. Once again, there was no breeze. She backed toward the hallway.

"Yoo-hoo."

Abigail jumped.

"Abigail?"

Stumbling, she headed for the front door, gathering her composure as she went. She pushed open a squeaky screen door and joined Sally on the porch.

"Hey, new neighbor, are you ready for dinner?" Sally's dangle earrings sparkled. "You've been busy." She craned her neck to peer up at the second story, nodding like an articulated toy. "Look at all those clean windows. I can smell the vinegar from here."

Sally's clean jasmine scent made Abigail only too aware of her sweaty and tired state. What she wanted was a soak in the tub and a cold glass of white wine. "About dinner, um, I appreciate the invitation but I wouldn't be good company tonight."

Sally's bracelets clanked as she waved her hands. "Exactly why you should come over. I know about rehabbing a house. Mine wasn't in as bad a shape as yours, but still." She tilted her head to the side and narrowed her eyes. "We're neighbors."

Abigail slumped against her railing. "I don't think—"

"You need to eat."

"I'm not sure I—" She swallowed and began again. "I don't have any clean clothes with me."

Sally's left hand waved dismissively. "What's a little dirt between neighbors? It'll just be the two of us. All you need to do is eat and relax."

Abigail's voice climbed into the upper registers. "Listen, could we make it—"

"I'll have a cold glass of wine waiting. You prefer a dry white, correct? My door will be open so just walk in." Sally turned and padded to her home, her verbal onslaught disappearing with her.

Rubbing her hands against her grimy jeans, Abigail replayed their conversation and wondered when she'd reach the eye of Hurricane Sally. She could swing a hammer with the best carpenter. Why couldn't she tell Sally "no"?

****

Her neighbor's door loomed. She'd never walked into someone's home without being greeted at the door by the owners. She shifted from foot-to-foot. Finally she knocked and cracked open the door. "Hello?"

"Come on in, the kitchen's straight back."

Abigail walked down the hallway then stopped in the kitchen doorway, mouth open. She'd dreamed about this room repeatedly and in detail, right down to the vented grill cook top. She shivered.

Sally waved her arm expansively toward the room furnished with warm-toned wood, bright colors, and comfortable furniture. "Come in, make yourself at home."

Senses whirling, Abigail floundered for an anchor then collapsed onto a wooden stool beside the cook top. True, her neighbor impressed her as a bit strange, well, really strange with her woo-woo speak and hippie clothes. Still, the house showed a side of Sally she could accept. This kitchen seemed like home.

Sally poured two glasses of wine. She handed one to Abigail, then attacked a pile of raw vegetables, chopping them efficiently between sips of her own wine.

Abigail sat quietly mulling her situation. Why would someone she didn't know treat her so well? The folks in her Charlotte apartment building hadn't spoken past "hello" much less asked her to dinner. They'd all kept to themselves. She'd been a little lonely, but understood the scene. Maybe she should have stayed in the city.

The aroma of vegetables sizzling in hot oil filled the room. Sally pushed them around the wok then stopped stirring. "You know, I didn't stop to ask if you like stir fry. I hope you don't mind. I'm pretty much a vegetarian."

Abigail's stomach growled in response.

Sally giggled. "Okay, that's a good answer. And just in time. Do you mind grabbing the wine bottle from the fridge? And bring the chiller along."

After they were settled and had begun eating, Sally looked at Abigail from over the rim of her wine glass. "I'm curious. What brought you to Blue Peak?"

Abigail's jaw froze in mid-bite. She knew she shouldn't have come here. A game of twenty questions was so not welcome. Talking to a stranger about the troubles that had prompted her relocation? Not tonight and maybe not for a long time.

Sally waved her fork in a tight circle. "You don't have to answer. It's just that this is a small town and everyone's curious. You know, a single woman buying a run-down home. Makes people wonder." Her bright eyes held an expectant expression.

"I, uh, I've always liked small towns. Plus, this house was in my price range."

"Why Blue Peak? It's a perfect town but an odd choice for a beautiful woman like you to make. I'd expect you to prefer Charlotte or Raleigh."

A portion of the truth would do. "It's close to Asheville, and Charlotte is easy to reach. I like the mountains, visited on vacation, and decided it would be a good place to settle someday."

"I get it," Sally plunked her fork down. "I came here to escape the world too." She smiled. "And then I found it."

Abigail shifted and rolled her shoulders. Sally's words touched too close.

"Don't worry. Blue Peak is the right place for you."

If Sally mentioned auras again she'd run straight out of there, no stopping.

Sally finished chewing swallowed and said, "We'll take care of you. You'll be just fine."

No one had used that warm tone with her in years. Abigail's emotions roiled. Her throat closed. The backs of her eyes burned. She didn't respond, but Sally picked up the conversation as if she didn't expect an answer.

They discussed local places of interest. Later, Abigail forced herself to leave for her furnished rental. She'd had fun after all. Perhaps Sally could be trusted, in time.

Chapter Three

The Collective Unconscious Café rang with chatter, cappuccino machine whooshes and music. Carlos hid in the kitchen. No need to take out a personals ad. He'd made a conscious decision to date and, bam. The *real* collective unconscious had telegraphed his decision to every single woman in the vicinity before he'd made one phone call. Damn it.

His coffee house held more than the normal number of women today. Unless they'd been coming here before and he hadn't noticed? Who knew. Double damn it.

A lot of guys would be salivating but the whole social scene gave him the dating hangover shakes. One Sierra in a lifetime had been more than enough. He'd lost more than a fiancée when she'd bailed. Her defection had sent him running from the career he loved. Mentoring students who sought him out here wasn't the same.

Deserting his haven, he slapped down a plate of food. "Order up!"

Female heads snapped up, all eyes looking his way. Shit. He felt like a quarterback with a cluster of defensive linebackers an inch away from sacking him. Enough. He'd get the hell out of there.

"Cover for me." Not giving his baristas time to answer, he ducked down the hall to his office, slamming the door behind him.

Henry looked up from the chew toy trapped between his paws. When no leash action occurred, he returned his attention to gnawing.

Carlos paced the room. Stupid. He couldn't hide back here for long. He outlined the pro and con arguments for dating.

The pro side won.

He'd look for the two women he'd decided on and toss a coin if they'd both shown today. Something told him he'd find a woman to date in his coffee house. Time to dive into the dating pool. Damn it.

****

Abigail reviewed her progress, excited she remained on track. She'd enjoyed dinner with Sally, who'd promised introductions to more people. Life rocked.

Even so, every hour brought more additions to a never-ending to-do list. She reminded herself this was her dream. Plus she'd invested a major chunk of her divorce settlement in this house. A familiar knot formed in her stomach. Her move had to work.

When she walked into the house after taking a lunch break, a heavy dose of pipe tobacco smoke spiked a coughing fit. She caught her breath.

"Is someone here?" Her eyes searched the room for anything extraordinary. Nothing jumped out at her, but her skin quivered as if she were being watched. She preset her phone with the emergency number then moved carefully through the house holding a pry bar, certain her unease wasn't caused by anything human. Finding herself alone, she shook off her fear and concentrated on her never-ending list.

****

"Hey, neighbor! Had a break, yet?"

Halfway to the door, Abigail called back a "Hello." Sally looked an eyeful today in a long red dress imprinted with purple moons and stars, dangle earrings, an armful of bracelets, and multiple necklaces. A sweet woman with no fashion sense.

"A break? I don't—"

"Come on, have a cup of coffee with me."

Here she goes. Sally, the original irresistible force on the move again. "I don't have time to spare."

Sally crossed her arms, raising her eyebrows. "Sure you do."

Did the woman never give up? She'd get nowhere on this job if Sally kept interrupting. "Look, I've got crews coming in and—"

"You need a break. Come on. Fifteen minutes won't hurt."

It really ticked her off when people didn't listen. She always listened politely. Was it too much to ask of others to do the same?

Crap, she'd missed that last part. What had Sally just said?

"The Collective Unconscious Café is a great coffee house run by a former psych professor at the college." She uncrossed her arms. "You've got to meet the owner, he's—" Sally stopped as abruptly as she'd started. She cocked her head as if listening to someone.

Abigail took a big breath, preparing to start her "thanks but no thanks" speech. "I appreciate your invitation but—"

"Great! Come on, I'll drive." Sally pulled Abigail toward her car.

Well, if nothing else, she'd get a ride in her dream car, collect her free coffee, and put Carlos firmly out of her mind.

****

They walked into the mouth-watering aroma of good coffee and warm muffins. Abigail took the business' measure. Wooden tables with mismatched chairs filled much of the front part of the room. Sunlight streamed in through the two large front windows, creating patterns on the scarred oak floors.

A large blackboard hung behind the counter fronted by several stools. Different color chalks were used to list the menu, more extensive than she'd expected. In addition to the large listing, a smaller board on an easel announced the day's coffee and luncheon specials.

Beside the counter was a glass-fronted bakery case holding a selection of muffins and scones. A cash register rested nearby, along with a rack of coffee-themed magnets.

They threaded their way through tables filled with chattering women. Abigail figured Carlos had something to do with those phenomena. His shoulders really filled out that vintage shirt he wore. Today's garb featured a pick-up truck theme.

"I think you and Carlos will like each other." Sally held up a hand, palm out and kept walking. "No, I'm not trying to set you up."

"Um, actually, I've already met him. And Henry."

"Oh, that's wonderful. Why didn't you say so? Did he offer to give you a hand at the house?"

"Not exactly."

Sally stopped close to the counter. "What do you mean, 'not exactly'? Was he rude? I can see by your blush that something happened."

"Sally, are you harassing my customers?"

Abigail's spine loosened when she heard his low voice. She pulled herself together, turned and faced the man who'd invaded her previous night's dreams.

His smile faded, and his jaw tightened. While she took inventory, his eyes narrowed and his hands clenched. Guess they hadn't shared the same dream.

He blew out a breath before saying, "Welcome to my business. See? That's the recommended response when people stop to help."

She pushed back the hair that had escaped her ponytail. "I don't need your help."

His fists rested on his hips. "I get that."

Sally interrupted. "One of you better tell me what happened."

"Nothing. A minor disagreement." Abigail hugged herself.

Carlos looked down his nose. "I noticed her," he pointed toward Abigail, "standing in her driveway holding a mop like a life line." His teeth clenched as he looked at her. He turned back to Sally. "I thought she needed assistance. Remind me to stop playing Good Samaritan."

"I can see you two got off on the wrong feet. How about starting over?" Sally's tone held a world of hope.

Abigail straightened her shoulders feeling as if she faced a firing squad. "Look, I'm sorry. I have a lot of work ahead of me and not much time to finish." She held out her right hand. "I'm willing to start over if you are."

He eyed her outstretched hand for a moment before meeting it. "Sure, sorry I butted in. I see you're a woman who can handle herself."

Abigail's hand tingled from their brief handshake, the one he'd ended abruptly, as if bitten. She'd chosen to live in Blue Peak and needed to make her decision work.

Plus, the aroma permeating the room made her salivate. Truly, nothing beat a great cup of coffee. A man who made fabulous smelling java couldn't be all bad, not all the time.

"So, sweetie," Sally said as she settled on a stool. "Don't scare off my new neighbor."

His posture relaxed. "I think we agreed to an initial misunderstanding. Abigail, or Abby?"

"Abigail." *As my mother never let me forget. Shortening my name to Abby would mean banishment from the family.* She dropped her arms to her sides.

He leaned against the counter. "Welcome to Blue Peak. I offered you a coffee on the house yesterday. Want to collect?"

His grin insinuated he offered more than coffee. Her pulse picked up until she reminded herself she had no time for men. She slid onto the stool next to Sally's.

"A large with a double shot of low-fat in a to-go cup, please." She smiled. "Will you tell me how you chose your business name?"

He called Abigail's order to the closest barista. His eyebrows lifted in a non-verbal question to Sally, who nodded. He called out another order. Obviously Sally was a regular here. Either that or the two of them were having a fling. Sally could easily attract a younger guy, even one young enough to be her son.

Pouring a mug for himself he answered, "The Collective Unconscious Café? Too many years teaching

27

psych, I guess. Plus, I've never met a pun I didn't love. The pairing of unconscious and coffee just worked for me." He took Abigail's coffee from the barista, placing it in front of her.

"Thank you for the coffee. And for the offer of help."

Carlos flashed her a smile and moved to help a customer after serving Sally.

She sipped coffee. Heaven in a cup. The caffeine had to be the reason her heart pounded. "Sally, I really should get back."

Sally slid down from the stool. "Sure, just a second." She patted Abigail's arm saying, "I'll be right back," then hurried toward the restroom.

"Wait! I'll come along." Her foot got caught in the stool. She felt herself toppling then a strong hold stopped her descent.

"You okay?" Carlos's voice sounded worried.

Abigail caught her breath. She gave a shaky laugh. "Sure. Thanks for stopping me from hitting the floor. That would've been embarrassing." She looked at his hand on her arm. His grasp felt as warm as a heating pad set on medium-high.

He pulled away from her. "Yeah, someone might have thought you were falling for me."

"You can't stop yourself from making puns, can you?"

He grimaced. "Not really." He blew out a breath. "Relax. Sally will be right back. Why don't you keep me company for a minute?"

She shrugged, but her pulse sped. *He's starting to look like a nice guy. Something's gonna prove me wrong, soon.*

"So what brings you to Blue Peak?" He wiped down the counter in front of her.

She gave her pat answer. "I visited on vacation. Seemed like a good place to live."

His visual assessment held her prisoner. Then he smiled. "This is a special town. People like to help each other out, be neighbors. It can stifle some. It's a balm to others."

She knew it. He remained pissed, and he didn't like her. Her lower lip trembled; she licked her lips. "You obviously think I don't belong here."

His hands stilled as his eyes settled on her mouth. "I didn't say that."

She wiggled on the stool, wishing he'd stop the doublespeak. "What are you saying?"

He shrugged. "Just making conversation. You want me to top that off for you?"

****

Carlos pondered the Abigail enigma as she left with Sally. He'd been right. A woman he could date had walked into his coffee house-Abigail. No doubt he was interested because she wasn't drooling over him. But still. Something about her caught his interest. He'd sensed it when he shook hands with her, a tangible pull. He'd let go, fast. Then he'd experienced it again when he'd grabbed her arm. Electricity and heat sucked when the sparks came from an indifferent woman.

Maybe her sweet ass hugged by worn jeans created the attraction. Yeah.

Her lips? Uh, huh. He'd had to drag his eyes away from her lips, especially that full lower one she'd been chewing. Yep, he needed to find a woman, one who had more on her mind than a ramshackle house and an aversion to friendly offers of help. He glanced at his watch. Kitchen duty time.

His heart stuttered when she'd almost fallen. Sure, she could have gotten hurt, and he'd hate that. She looked like someone who'd been hurt in too many ways already.

He pulled on his "Licensed to Dill" apron before loading the dishwasher, recalling their conversation. Abigail wore old work clothes, her hair was a mess, and she hadn't used cosmetics. She looked directly at the person she spoke with and didn't mince words. Besides that, her determination to succeed shone clear.

Carlos straightened with the dish detergent in his hand. Now he understood. Abigail acted differently from any other woman he'd dated. She was the new, and she'd snared his attention. Just his bad luck that she didn't seem the type who could handle casual.

****

Sally danced out of the coffee house as Abigail plodded alongside, her head down. She should have grabbed another large coffee to accompany her long list of chores.

She listened half-heartedly while Sally spun stories. Did Abigail have a small town personality? She thought she did. Obviously, Carlos disagreed. Life here sure didn't fit her expectations.

"Thanks for coming with me."

Abigail smiled politely. "Thanks for getting me out of the house."

Sally stopped and examined her face. "You're working too hard. Life should be fun."

Abigail sighed. "I'm pretty goal-oriented. That turns some people off."

Sally gave her a sidelong glance. "Did Carlos say something stupid? If he did, I'll kick his butt."

"Carlos?" Abigail slowed. "No, I was thinking about you. I don't even know Carlos."

The older woman turned to face her, walking backward. "Would you like to?"

She tripped, but looking back, didn't see any uneven pavement. "What? No! I've got way too much on my plate to get involved in a romance."

A small smile hovered over Sally's lips. "Are you sure? I know Carlos is free."

"Then you date him." Her stomach knotted with the thought.

Sally laughed. "He spooks you, doesn't he?" She laid a finger against her cheek. "That's good. Very good."

Abigail's thoughts were colored with bewilderment. "You've seen my house. I really don't have—"

Sally stopped walking and touched her arm like a bird landing on a wire. "I'm free. Would you like some help?"

"Oh, no, you've done enough." Abigail's face heated with the unintended criticism. "That is, I mean—"

She tilted her head. "It's okay, I understand what you mean."

Abigail's shoulders fell with her exhale. "Maybe I can help you in return."

"This isn't tit-for-tat, neighbors help each other." Sally laughed. "You haven't lost your big city ways, yet. Give us time and pretty soon you'll fit right in."

She hoped that was true. She had a lot riding on her

investment.

****

Abigail scanned her home as she approached from the street after Sally dropped her off. A flash of movement in the bedroom window nabbed her attention. The curtains shifted in the still afternoon air. Closing her eyes tight, she opened them and looked again. No movement.

"Dang, I'd better cut back on my coffee intake. I'm seeing things." She looked around glad no one had caught her talking to herself. When she entered, she couldn't find her project list.

"Well, that's strange. I'm sure I left it right here." She searched the house and returned to the kitchen. A glimpse of paper under the refrigerator caught her eye. Ignoring the question of how the list had moved, she grabbed it and began making notes.

Cool air washed over her along with a low-pitched masculine voice. "Hello, girlie." A pause. "Have you decided to listen?"

The quiet words came from right beside her. She scanned the empty kitchen. The hair on her nape stirred as the tinkling sound of the dining room's chandelier reached her.

She took a deep breath and said, "I don't believe in ghosts. Go away." The quiet took on a somber quality as she waited for a reaction.

Abigail exhaled with a grunt. "This is nuts."

She inserted her ear buds and boosted the volume on her media player. No one else was there and she didn't hear phantom words. She didn't have time for fantasies.

Chapter Four

A Jack Russell terrier ran alongside a young man riding a bike. They'd appeared over the hill as Abigail settled on a bench outside the Collective Unconscious Café. Joggers and early morning walkers greeted her on their way past. The scent of hot coffee and fresh bakery escaped when customers hurried into the coffee house, stimulating her taste buds. She straightened, preparing to rise.

Whoa, girl, hold up a minute. She slumped against the bench. Sure, she'd planned on buying a gift card to thank Sally for dinner, but that didn't account for her increased pulse rate. She reluctantly faced the truth. The promise of a rare Carlos smile drew her more than the excuse of purchasing a gift card.

But would a smile be enough? She sure didn't have time for more. And Rich, well that'd been a lesson and a half. She'd trusted him, thinking he'd been her best friend. He'd been her only friend. He'd laughed at her dreams of having their own home instead of fixing up places for other people while they lived out of boxes in an apartment.

Then he'd said he couldn't be married anymore. She'd asked for reasons but he hadn't given any. She'd barely moved out before he had another woman living with him. Replaced after almost ten years in less than two weeks. Damn. She rubbed her chest. That still hurt.

Hadn't Rich told her more than once that she couldn't get anything done without him? Renovating her new house, settling in Blue Peak, were her acid tests. Now wasn't the time to fall for good looks and a killer smile. She had a lot to prove, starting with herself.

Abigail rose, dusted off her butt, and looked over the square. Her taste buds clamored for Carlos's coffee, but they'd have to wait. She wouldn't return until she knew exactly what she wanted and why.

****

Carlos looked outside. Abigail still sat on his bench. He and his two baristas were working steadily with the normal morning rush, but he'd noticed her immediately.

He shook his head while preparing a large cappuccino. Abigail was wound way too tight for his comfort. Plus his mother wore a complacent smile every time he'd seen her lately. So why couldn't he move on? There were plenty of available women who weren't so wounded.

Exchanging greetings and a joke with the next customer in line, he worked on an order. What bothered him about Abigail anyway? Outside of her blonde looks, he'd avoided that type of hands-off woman. She made him feel—

His hands, heart, and brain crashed to a halt.

Holy crap. It was so damn obvious. His hands moved into motion. She made him feel. He hadn't done much of that since Sierra.

Hot coffee splattered over his "Real Men Bake" apron. Damn it, time to pull his brain back into the northern hemisphere. If he needed an omen, getting burned said it all.

She walked off without glancing his way. That tingle of awareness was his and his alone. Shit. He plastered on a smile for the next customer and rubbed the nape of his neck. He'd had his fill of useless conjecture. His customers needed coffee. He had a business to run. Students to mentor. He'd call the two women he'd chosen for dates today. Why stop with one female?

****

Brown paper covered the front windows of Good Vibes but an "Open" sign hung on the door. Although certain her house had a ghost, Abigail decided to consult with Sally about the cold and whispers. Sally wouldn't need to know that Abigail had conversed with her grandparents after they died. That had been her imagination, according to her mother. She took a deep breath and stepped inside.

A mixed fragrance greeted her. She picked out lavender and mint, but the other aromas escaped definition. Water gurgled in a fountain beside the front door, and she received an impression of warmth in the large room. Abigail noted filled bookshelves and a card rack before Sally bustled to her.

"Welcome, I'm glad you're here. Come, let's sit down."

They moved to a seating area furnished with a couch and two chairs around a low table.

"I hope I didn't interrupt you," Abigail said, spotting several papers holding sketches.

"No problem. I was working on window design plans for the Summer Solstice. You know, the first day of summer and the longest day of the year. More time to party." She performed a shoulder shimmy. "I want to have it in place by this weekend."

She cleared her throat. "Hey, enough about business. How can I help you?"

Abigail inhaled through her nose. "Can you tell me about the people who lived in my house? I didn't meet the seller, only the lawyer with Power of Attorney who closed for the estate."

"Gordon and Lydia Wilkinson. I didn't spend as much time with them as I should have. I'm ashamed to say I spent most of my time building the store business."

Abigail's hopes faded. "Oh, so you didn't know them well."

"I did, but not for long." Her fingers formed a steeple. "Lydia had cancer. Gordon brought in nurses and housekeepers when she worsened. He fell apart after she died. I'd see him when he'd walk out for his daily paper, usually dressed in his bathrobe. He didn't live long after she died, maybe a year. The house went downhill really fast after she passed. He tried to keep up, but I think the house and garden mourned Lydia."

Abigail didn't stop to censor her comments, ignoring her personal beliefs about houses owning spirits. Instead, she spoke the standard response everyone had given her when she'd said essentially the same thing. "That's a little out there, don't you think?"

Sally shrugged. "I've seen and heard odder stuff. Anyway, their only child Julia put the house on the market. She never came back to attend the estate sale or to take any of the furnishings, not even for the funerals. From what I've heard, she left here and never returned. Don't know her reasons."

Putting her finger against her cheek, Sally seemed lost in thought. "Gordon was sweet, always treated me with courtesy and respect. And believe me, not everyone has over the years. He always looked so lost there at the end. He lived longer than I expected after his wife passed."

They grew quiet with the thought of a link that devoted.

Abigail's heart ached. Would she ever find that kind of love?

Sally roused herself. "I hope that helped. Did you have any other questions?"

"Did either of them smoke?"

"Gordon. He always had a lit cigarette or pipe."

The knowledge settled into Abigail's bones, and she experienced a sense of exultation. So. She'd been right. Her home hosted a ghost. She wasn't crazy, and her mother had been wrong. Ghosts did exist and this one wanted to communicate with her. Her throat muscles clenched. If only she'd continued contact with her grandmother. She'd have help on the other side. She doubted she could figure this out on her own.

The women looked up when the door opened.

Sally stood and waved. "Carlos, hi sweetie." She moved to greet him.

Abigail hid her heated face. Great. The one person she'd just decided she couldn't see.

Sally said, "A thermos of coffee for me?"

Carlos's deeper voice rumbled a reply. Crap, crap, crap. She had to leave. If she scooted around the angel display, she could make it to the door without having to squeeze past Carlos.

No luck. Sally caught her arm. "You're not leaving

so soon? Look who just stopped by with a treat. I know you love his...coffee."

He smiled. "I'm pretty handy with a measuring tape if you need someone to hold the dumb end. I know my way around a hammer, too."

She tightened her jaw. Did he think she wasn't smart or strong enough to do the work on her own? He sounded more like Rich every time they spoke. He'd take over her project if she let him.

Abigail tamped down her anger and injected a note of regret into her voice. "I really have to go. Thanks again for the information, Sally. I'll come back soon." She nodded at him. "Carlos."

****

"Well that was a waste of time." Carlos ran his fingers through his hair. "I made nice like you asked and got blown off."

"She likes you."

He snorted.

"Attraction glowed all over her aura. And don't you snort at me, young man. I know what I saw, even if you don't believe me." Her head tilted to the side. "You'll make pretty grandbabies together."

"Earth to Mom." Damn it all. She could still make him feel ten years old. She'd keep that power as long as she lived. "You won't get grandbabies if Abigail runs the other way every time she sees me."

She clapped. "Oh, good. You're finally starting to see things my way."

He shook his head. "No, I'm not. Your grandchildren are not on my agenda. I'd just like to learn more about her. Let things flow. Damn it. Now I sound like you."

"You're the psych professor. I'm sure you've figured out that someone undermined her confidence. She came here to prove herself." Sally placed a finger over her mouth. Her gaze found the ceiling.

"I may be the psychologist but you taught Women's Studies for years. Why don't you tell me where I'm going wrong here?" He sighed. "I can't believe I just asked my mother for help with a woman."

She narrowed her eyes at him. "You *should* ask me. Teaching psychology and practicing it are two different things. Not only did you blow it with Abigail, you haven't given me what I most want. Grandchildren. Before I'm too frail to hold them. A daughter-in-law is optional if you don't believe in marriage."

"Oh, hell. I hate when you pull out that old guilt trip. You taught me how to identify manipulators. Don't you think I can peg your attempts?" He hugged her to his side. "Besides, frail my butt. You'll probably hike the Appalachian Trail when you celebrate your hundredth birthday. And support me every step of the way."

Carlos released her and blew out a breath. "Look, I just want a chance to talk with Abigail. Nothing more and nothing less, Miss Free-Spirit-Women's-Libber. Will you help me?"

"What I want sweetie, is for you to move on from Sierra. I never did like that woman. I got bad vibes the moment we met. Are you ready to let go of the hurt she put on you? Because I won't help you with Abigail if you're going to dump her like all the others."

"Sierra, yeah, I admit she did a number on me. But I can deal." He hesitated in committing more. "I just want to know if that's really hope I see behind the sadness in her eyes. Abigail's a puzzle, Mom."

"And I know how you love mysteries. Besides, I can see both your auras. I'll help."

He groaned. "Enough with the metaphysical pseudo-science."

She shook her finger. "You got more from your dad than just your looks. He didn't listen to me, either." She transferred her glance to the window. "I see a line out the door at your place. You'd better run."

They hugged and he left. She'd done it again. Mentioned his father then shut down. She'd never bad-mouthed the man, but hadn't encouraged questions. He'd sensed the topic hurt her and didn't pursue it, but he had questions. He knew his parents had met at Woodstock and his dad had been a musician. He'd put off pursuing answers but perhaps now he should find information on his missing parent. Right after he solved the puzzle Abigail presented.

****

Abigail parked in her driveway after going out for dinner. She remained behind the wheel, watching the sun fall behind the trees. Hours later, the memory of her interaction with Carlos still made her heart race and her juices run. Even new to town, she'd overheard the stories. He'd gone through a dating frenzy, dropping most of the women after a date or two. Just like her ex had before they'd met and married. Another good-looking man did not figure in her immediate plans. Abigail corrected herself. Another *man* was not in her plans, immediate or even further out. She'd been hurt for the last time.

She climbed from the truck. Even if she lived alone with a houseful of cats, no make that a dog because she'd get exercise walking it, she wouldn't put her heart out there again. No way.

The sight from her kitchen doorway stopped her cold. A steady drip, almost a stream of water ran from the faucet. A pail she didn't remember leaving in the sink had stopped the drain. Water covered the floor in a thin sheet.

Abby slogged to the sink, twisting the faucet tighter. She stilled, listening for noises. The house was totally quiet. Unnaturally quiet. As if it waited for her reaction.

No, not the house. A *being* in the house. There, a cool touch on her neck. Her skin puckered with chill bumps.

"Gordon? Gordon Wilkinson, is that you? If you made this mess, I'll get you."

The chill left her neck then the room warmed. Her sense of being watched disappeared.

Abigail grabbed a mop. This would put a hurt on her priorities. A brief whiff of tobacco smoke teased her senses. It smelled fresh. She ignored it. Her imagination worked overtime, again. Enough already. Something sounded at the edge of her hearing, an echo of light footsteps. She reached for her phone, ready to dial nine-one-one on her way out the door.

"Lydia where are you? You promised me you'd come meet me."

Abigail stiffened. She had her answer. The ghost *was* Gordon Wilkinson.

The low murmur sounded again, drawn out this time, pitiful. "Lydia? I need you."

She stilled. Cold air wrapped around her.

The voice spoke at her ear. "I can't do this for

Lydia alone. Help me find the letters."

Her frigid muscles contracted with tension, ears straining to hear her only active sense.

"Lydia, please." The words faded away, as did the cold.

After a moment she shook herself like a dog after a bath.

Letters? Her ghost had a mission.

Chapter Five

Abigail stood, water lapping around her shoes. A wave of cold air bathed her, followed by a strong tobacco aroma. The sensation of long fingers trailed across her face. Shivers traveled her spinal column.

"G-g-gordon Wilkinson? You are here, right? Not some other ghost?"

She choked on a deep breath. If her ghost answered, she wouldn't hear him over her raspy breaths. The chandelier tinkled softly.

She heard a low gurgling sound and transferred her gaze to the sink. Pipes moaned a short warning just before water gushed from the faucet and swirled down the drain. She squealed, "Oh. My. God. OHMYGOD. Oh, Oh, Oh!!"

The mop fell from her nerveless fingers. Abigail's feet refused her demand to move. A scraping sound attracted her; the pail rattled back and forth as the water shut off. That couldn't be real. Then the mop rose into the air. All under its own—or a ghost's—steam.

The pail and mop moved around the room. Her blood pressure moved to overload. Somehow the now synchronized movements looked familiar. Her eyes widened. Of course. The actions were a parody of that old cartoon of a mouse wearing a sorcerer's hat.

Abigail's muscles thawed. She raced for the door, not stopping until she reached her truck. She clawed at the door. Damn. Her keys were inside the house. She walked to the end of her drive and stood under the street lamp.

Quivering, she hyperventilated wishing she had a paper bag to blow into. She twitched as if her nervous system were direct wired into a generator. The damn ghost had a strange sense of humor. Her clammy hands clenched and unclenched to a nervous rhythm, unable to hold still. Her over-stimulated senses heard nails scratching against the sidewalk. Now what? A werewolf? She chose not to look, fearful of what she'd see.

Soft fur brushed against her legs, a cold nose pushed into her palm. She jumped then recognized Henry's familiar form. She swallowed. "Hey, big guy, how'd you get here?"

Carlos. He'd arrive soon, never far from his dog. Could this night worsen?

"What's wrong? You look like you've seen a ghost."

Yep. The night could suck. Abigail turned. "Ghost? Not likely."

"I'm not big on the unproven stuff, but ghosts are a possibility in this old town. Did you know Civil War troops passed through here? A battle took place about ten miles out of town. Yep, if I had to choose, I'd accept ghosts over auras and all that crap." He tilted his head. "I suppose you share Sally's beliefs, considering where I last met you."

"Where we last met? Oh, Good Vibes."

"So, can I scare off a big, bad ghostie for you?"

"Yes."

"Yes?" He studied her face under the streetlight's

glare. "You're shaking. What happened?"

Abigail described the flickering lights and voice, but left out the dancing mop, stopped-up sink, and tobacco odors. She shivered.

He removed his light-weight jacket, placing it around her shoulders. His voice pitched low he said, "Like I said, I don't believe in much of the stuff called supernatural, but you look upset. And tired. Perhaps you've been working too hard."

"You don't believe me." Why did that not surprise her? She'd been called a liar and punished for telling her mother she spoke with her grandparents after their death. She'd hid her experiences for years, pushing down what she'd believed real. Rich had laughed at her "fantasies" about homes having a spirit. Now Carlos did the same. Well, tough. She knew what she'd sensed was real to her. The hell with everyone else. Everyone except Sally. She was sure Sally understood.

Abigail gulped, her throat tight and sandy. "I'm fine so you can leave now." She pulled off his coat and handed it to him. "Thanks for stopping."

He dropped his jacket and placed his hands on her upper arms. "Will you be okay?"

She stepped from his reach. "Yes, thanks again."

"I get the feeling you think I'm discounting your experience. Sorry."

She shrugged. "I've learned men only see what they want to see."

He didn't reply the same could be said about women, which surprised her. She'd looked for a button to push because his calm demeanor ticked her off. Now he studied her face like she held a mystery.

"I know Sally's not home tonight, but you should

45

talk with her tomorrow. Just because I don't believe in ghosts...well, I know she's studied the supernatural for years."

Abigail nodded. "Sure thing. Thanks." She bent to pet Henry, who had plastered himself against her leg. "Night, big guy."

Carlos rubbed the back of his neck. "Yeah, well, guess we'll get out of your hair. That is, you'll be okay, right? You're not staying here tonight, are you?"

"I'm fine." What, did he think she'd jump in his lap because she'd been frightened? Jackass.

She turned on her heel and strode to her home, stopping at the stairs. Like she'd want his—or any man with strong arms at her side. Damn right she did, at least to get her keys and close up the house. She'd have to control her hormones because she wouldn't hook up with another man like Rich.

****

Carlos remembered the feel of her upper arms, warm and smooth as she disappeared in the black pool of shadows in her yard. No wonder her eyes held a wounded look. Some asshole had done a number.

He could help her with that. If nothing else, she needed a friend. He'd have to slowly gain her trust, but he had patience.

She'd said she'd seen flickering lights before the power had been turned on. He'd noticed lights periodically over the last year, usually when walking Henry right before bedtime. Carlos had figured kids were goofing around outside. He'd checked for signs of entry or underage drinking then. There were none, so he hadn't bothered the police.

Carlos stopped walking, ignoring Henry's pull at

the end of his leash. What if the flickers were caused by something else?

He rolled his neck to loosen the sudden tightness.

Nah.

****

Abigail fought shakiness and for control of her truck. Her jello-like legs barely pushed in the heavy clutch, her weak arms fought to engage the transmission. She parked, finally, in her apartment's lot and struggled inside.

She collapsed on the bathroom floor, the tears she'd restrained flowing softly then turning into heavy sobs. Fear, anger, grief, she couldn't delineate between the emotions. Hiccupping, she pulled herself upright and ran a bath.

Hot water lapped around her as she lowered into an aromatic tub full of hot water and bubbles. Thoughts drifted, following the steamy tendrils rising from the bath water.

Her home. Her new ghost-filled home. She tensed then forced her muscles to relax one by one. Mr. Wilkinson would leave when he'd completed his mission. She'd keep working on the house. Abigail wouldn't be scared off, couldn't really afford to allow that to happen. She'd figure out a way to work with the ghost.

"Yes," she whispered, "I can do this."

Her traitorous subconscious pulled her mother's face to mind. She cringed, remembering angry shouts.

"You're a liar. You can't talk to my parents. They're dead. Dead, do you hear me? Stop making up stories."

Her hand covered the phantom pain of the slap

she'd received, trying to forget the argument that night, when she'd heard her grandparents for the last time.

"If my parents were talking with anyone, it would be to me, not you. You're nothing more than a little crazy person looking for attention. If you tell me one more time that your grandmother is watching over you, the next thing you'll see is the inside of a looney bin. Get it? Now stop. I mean it. Stop those stories right now."

She'd turned away from the loving feeling accompanying their spectral visits and refused to heed her grandparents' voices. Abigail blew out a long breath. Now she knew her mother had been mired in grief. Grief and guilt for not treating her own parents with more love. Sometimes she wondered why her mother couldn't show affection. Goodness knows Abigail's grandparents were warm, gracious people.

Regardless, now she faced having to speak with a dead person. She didn't think she could. She'd pushed down her abilities for so long, she didn't believe helping Mr. Wilkinson was possible. So far, every time she'd called to him, he'd disappeared. Fat lotta good avoidance did either of them. How did you go about contacting someone who wasn't related to you?

Sally knows. Talking with Sally meant sharing her secret. Did she have a choice?

"I'm not going to backtrack," she breathed. Her mother's voice sounded in her head, reminding her not to air her linen in public. She'd heard those words once too often. Perhaps she should break out of her mold. Her breath caught. She'd already taken the first steps to starting a new life. Time to think in new ways too.

She looked down. When had she lost so much

weight? Why did she think she still needed to diet? Those were her mother's standards, not hers.

Adhering to her mother's insistence on maintaining physical facades wasn't the only change she'd make. Yeah. Time to discover her true self.

Damn it, she'd enjoy her new home and hometown. She'd known when she had first seen the mid-sized college town named Blue Peak that the location was meant for her. Nothing would stop her from her dreams this time.

Nothing.

Chapter Six

Carlos nodded absently at a patron as he wiped the counter again. He refused to admit he'd stationed himself at the best spot to see the door on purpose. Abigail didn't cause his restlessness. She was another customer, that's all. One he hoped he hadn't alienated last night.

But, really, ghosts? Her episodes could be easily explained. Overwork. Exhaustion. Forgetfulness. All caused by the stress of renovation. Plus, lots of old houses had strange creaks and moans. Still, he'd seen lights flickering at night. Kids. Had to be kids goofing around.

He put elbow grease into polishing the counter to a more glass-like substance. Time to screw his head back on. His crew sporadically threw him questioning looks. He acted like a horny teenager for cripes' sake

Good thing he'd asked Jillian Colvin out. He needed an undamaged woman. Someone who knew the score and just wanted to share a few laughs. Some hot sex. Nothing more. Abigail Stephens was not that woman.

He turned to pour a refill when the atmosphere changed. Abigail had walked in. Turning around, his glance flew to her like a champion darter's throw to the double twenty.

He drank in her presence thinking maybe he should

50

reconsider dating Jillian, because Abigail's smile hit him hard. He shook his head. That's exactly why he needed to see someone else. Abigail was trouble in capital letters. Nutty, too, given she thought she'd heard a ghost speak.

But those bib overalls she wore made him wonder what kind of curves ... no, he wouldn't go there. He snapped his perusal back to her face, only to focus on her full lips. His gaze snail paced toward her eyes.

"Good morning, Abigail. What's your pleasure this morning?" She looked refreshed, like a load had dropped off her shoulders last night. Ah, yes, maybe because she'd shared her fantasies with him. He'd rather listen to her sexual daydreams than supernatural claptrap. Yep, Jillian looked better and better.

"Hi. How about a large coffee of the day? Oh, and seeing as how you're the Dude with the Food, I want some bakery."

He looked down. Yep, that was the saying on the apron he'd fastened over his favorite vintage Italian shirt this morning.

"Muffins," she said. "Two, no, make that four."

Carlos crooked an eyebrow. "You getting ready to do some serious sugar-fueled work at the house?" What an idiot. He knew better than to question a woman's relationship with sugar, or to get between sucrose and her.

Abigail's lips quirked. "Yes I am, but these are social muffins."

"So you want the kind that get along together? How do you know they're sociable? Or do you just take a chance when you pick them out? A muffin fight could be nasty. All those raisins." His thoughts jumped to a different sort of raisin'.

Abigail's laughter strangled. "Um, yes, um, well, I'm, uh...I thought I'd stop by Good Vibes this morning and Sally mentioned that she loves your muffins. I mean these muffins."

Blushing looked cute on her. "So have you made a choice?" *Pick me.*

"Ah, there are too many to decide. Do you know Sally's favorites?"

"Of course. It'll be a minute." He busied himself folding and lining a cardboard pastry box with parchment. He looked over his shoulder. "I'll put in two for Sally. Why don't you decide what you'd like for yourself?"

"Oh, just give me two of the blueberry."

Carlos snuck a look at her through the display glass window. She had more on her mind than picking bakery. Not his concern.

He turned with a neatly wrapped carton in his hands. "Here you go. I guarantee satisfaction with everything I offer." He quashed a smile, kicking himself for making a sexually charged statement. So not going there, not with a woman who didn't even shorten her name to Abby. What was up with the formal name and masculine clothes, anyway?

No response to either his offer or his silent question. "Would you like coffee to go?" At her blank stare he said, "I can lend you a thermos."

"Great, thanks. Just fill it with Sally's favorite, please."

She was probably pissed because he blew her off last night. If he told her he'd seen lights at her home, she'd think he played her. But he couldn't let her leave before he apologized. He'd make that effort for any customer.

Placing the thermos next to the pastry box he said, "My treat."

"Oh, but I couldn't—"

His jaw jutted. He quickly smoothed his expression into a smile. "Oh, but you could." He pushed the box toward her. "It's my apology for acting like a jackass last night. My mom drove me crazy, taking me along on her ghost hunting trips when I was a kid. I should have been happy, staying up until midnight, but waiting for nothing bored me. I'd rather have been home, reading."

Her forehead crinkled. Did she not know he was Sally's son or had he said something even dumber?

"Thanks for your gift today, and for your apology. I must have looked crazy to you."

"Crazy attractive." Damn it. He shouldn't flirt.

Her face reddened. "Uh, thanks again. Bye." She grabbed her packages and turned away.

A strange impulse had him belie his scruples. "Remember, I'm available. Anytime. For any reason."

****

Abigail mentally kicked herself as she hurried out the door. Why did she teeter on the verge of melted goo-ness around Carlos? He was another handsome guy to avoid. Her steps slowed. Had she really been avoiding guys? She shook her head. No, she'd been busy at her interim job in Charlotte and had tons of work here.

Yeah, he was gorgeous. She'd observed his interactions with customers and employees while she'd waited in line. He'd been unfailingly polite to everyone. So what. He most likely thought her an idiot. He apologized. Period.

When he'd teased her about muffin fights, she'd visualized him baring his tight, nude buttocks for her. The mental picture of his eyes gleaming with promise had almost knocked her over. She must have been standing too close to the coffee machine considering the heat that had hit her body. At thirty-five, she was too young for hot flashes. How had she answered his question? For that matter, what had he asked her?

As if he'd show interest in a woman who wore overalls and work boots. She'd promised herself she wouldn't get involved with a man yet here she walked, salivating over Carlos. Where was her focus? Her discipline? She had a house to renovate, a new career to establish, and a limited budget. All of those goals had to be met to build her new life in Blue Peak.

Dreams, she had dreams. She didn't have time for a man. Not even the Dreamboat Carlos.

The Good Vibes' window sparkled. Abigail peered through the glass and around a bright paper sun. Seeing a customer inside, she caught Sally's attention and cocked her eyebrows. Sally waved her in.

She placed the muffins and thermos on the counter. Then she moved to the neatly labeled bookshelves.

After the customer left, Sally hugged Abigail. "You know you're welcome here any time. You don't have to bring a gift. You're enough all by yourself."

Abigail's breath caught in her throat. She blinked rapidly. She'd made the right decision to move to this small town. Once the ghost left everything would get better.

They sat down. "What's happening at the house?"

Abigail braced herself. "Gordon Wilkinson hasn't

left."

"Really? I'm not surprised. I've seen lights flickering in the house and in the yard over the past year or so." She leaned closer. "Tell me more."

Abigail rattled off the ghostly doings to date. "I'll take all the help I can get."

Sally straightened. "Gordon Wilkinson was supposed to handle some letters, he didn't, so now he's stuck. Common story." She touched Abigail's shoulder. "Are you okay?"

"I…yes, I am. Henry and Carlos arrived right after I ran from the house. Carlos suggested I talk with you."

Sally squeezed her shoulder. "I'm here to help."

A sudden lump filled Abigail's throat. Swallowing around it she said, "Thanks. I'm not sure what I'll do next, but I'm not leaving. I can't...the money...I hoped you could give me some ideas."

Sally sat back. "My intuition tells me you have to handle this situation."

Crap. Sally must be referring to psychic skills. Of course, she wouldn't mean anything normal by "my intuition." But wait. Abigail could change her ways. Her old beliefs weren't helping her adapt.

"He hasn't talked with me and I think the letters were discarded. The house had been cleared but for the drapes, an attic room full of odds and ends, and outdated appliances. Not much paperwork." She toyed with the idea of disclosing her past but backed down. "Look, do you have any ideas at all about what I should do?"

Sally sat quietly, with that air of listening Abigail had noticed before. What did she hear? And who spoke? Questions for another time.

"Gordon needs your help. It's your path and it's not for me to do more than support you. So I can't tell you exactly how to find the letters but I do know they concern his daughter. And you. They're in the house somewhere. I'm not hearing anything more."

Abigail looked at her hands. Damned letters again. "If I don't find the letters, will Gordon be able to move on? Or will he be stuck here?"

She shrugged. "Sorry, I can't say."

Abigail wasn't surprised. So far, nothing about this ghost assistant work had been easy.

****

"I see you came back to challenge the ghost." Carlos and Henry walked toward her from the driveway.

She straightened from repairing a step, her hand at the small of her back. "You didn't have to check on me." After a slight pause she added, "But thanks."

He noted the hesitation and pause. Carlos hoped his thoughtless words hadn't caused those reactions, but better to keep Abigail at arm's length. He'd had his first date with Jillian and decided to repeat the experience. No sex yet, but not because she hadn't offered.

"Henry and I walk here all the time. We live just a few blocks away. This is our turf, right Henry?" He patted the dog.

A small dumpster, filled to three-quarters sat in front of the detached garage. How did she accomplish so much on her own? She needed help. "You're really kicking butt here."

Her frown made him think she suspected him of who-knew-what.

"No, really, I can see progress. Dumpsters don't fill

themselves. The windows look clean. Ah, I'll have to take your word on anything else."

She smiled. Good. Smiles were good. Step one in his plan to make her his friend. That's all they could be. Friends.

"You bucking for detective? Isn't that the line from old police television shows?"

His neck muscles relaxed. "Sure. Another line is, 'I need some help with the case.'"

Her smile faltered. Shit.

She positioned herself at Henry's head and knelt. "How's my favorite dog tonight?" She petted the dog for a few moments, murmuring what sounded like nonsense to his ears. She looked up at him from under her eyelashes. Her eyes were amazing. Damn it. He shouldn't notice.

Abigail swallowed. "Thank you and Henry for stopping last night."

Now his throat was dry. "Even though I told you ghosts don't exist?"

She shifted and rose. "I spoke with Sally. She's very helpful."

"Look, I can't help you with ghosts, but I do know my way around a hammer."

"Thanks. I'll keep you in mind."

His control chafed. Stubborn woman. He could see she had a truckload of work without looking hard or long. Asking for help didn't cost anything, well not for most. Abigail saw a high cost where others didn't hesitate. The thought made him push when he should have walked.

"Really, Henry and I work cheap. A few dog bones will do."

She grinned. "And how do I pay Henry?"

"You'll have to ask him."

Chapter Seven

The next morning Abigail sipped hot coffee while considering Sally's words from the day before. How do you help a soul move on? Maybe she should rent *Ghost,* not that she had time or the equipment to watch a movie. Where the heck were those letters hidden?

"Gordon, if you're listening, I understand I'm supposed to help you, but I'm not happy about this situation. Not at all. I bought a house not a phantom ranch."

No answer, not even a whiff of stale tobacco.

"I don't have time to coddle you, so either start communicating—nicely—or stop messing with me. I've about had it with your silly poltergeist action. You hear me?"

Nothing. Either Gordon didn't consider women as equals or he was stubborn. With her luck? Both.

She drained her cup. No way she'd allow a dead former owner to renege on turning over full occupancy. Maybe she'd get lucky and find those damn letters today.

"Hey, cutie. Got some fresh fruit for you." Sally's voice echoed down the hall.

"Come in, the door's open."

"Nope, sorry, but you've got a mess going and I'm dressed for work."

She met Sally and took the bowl teeming with

fresh berries. "Yum. Thanks."

"How're you doing?"

"Paint crew coming in today."

"So why the icky face?"

Abigail sighed. "They had a bigger job reschedule and can't give me a full week. I'm hoping they can finish most of my interior, at least the first floor and stairway. I hate to leave things hanging."

"Well, girl, the Universe wants you here. I bet you'll get the work done faster than you expect. You can bank that bet."

Sally hadn't seen jobs fall apart the way she had. A renovation gone bad wasn't pretty. "I'm glad they didn't back out. I wanted the painting done before the hardwood refinishers arrive."

"Why worry about your schedule? You've got friends. You've got skills. Use them."

Her list was already full, now it headed toward overload. Pulling in unskilled people to work on her dream house? Asking for trouble, guaranteed.

Sally shook her head, as if hearing Abigail's thoughts. "Your friends are more skilled than you know. Don't forget I rehabbed my house, did a bunch of the work myself. Carlos knows his way around tools. I'm telling you, the Universe has plans for you. Fasten your seat belt, 'cause you're in for a ride."

She popped a berry in her mouth to avoid answering.

Sally shifted her feet. "Gotta go. Want to have dinner tonight?"

More time away from the job. Oh, what the hell? "Sounds great. What time?"

"How about six thirty? We'll make it an early

night."

"Where?"

"My house." Sally waved her hand. "Don't worry. You can cook for me once you're up and running."

"I'll bring wine."

Now what the hell else could push her off schedule today?

****

"Damn, it's cold in here." Abigail checked the thermostat. Off.

Uh, oh. She didn't need the ghost coming around now. Not with the paint crew here. She pushed aside the plastic covering the kitchen door. Warm in the hallway.

A tobacco aroma hit her nostrils when she ducked behind the plastic. No raspy voice in her ear. Not yet. She hated getting ambushed.

"Mr. Wilkinson? Are you here? If you're here, I'd like to speak with you." Her whisper sounded ragged. If anyone heard her they'd call the local sanitarium.

"Mr. Wilkinson?" No response, even the tobacco aroma had dissipated. He had to be here given the cold.

"Listen ghostie, I told you before. This is my house now and I'm sick of your pranks. Why are you here?" She looked over her shoulder at the doorway, reminding herself to keep her voice down.

"If you don't tell me why you're here, I can't help you now, can I?"

Without warning, an angry voice bellowed in her head. "Help me? You thoughtless puppy. You're ruining my house. Why are you throwing everything in the trash?"

"Wwwhhaaat?"

"The house I worked to give Lydia is being

destroyed. Don't you have any sense, girl?"

She gulped. Her legs shook. She inhaled past dry lips then straightened her shoulders.

"Mr.—" She cleared her throat and began again. "Mr. Wilkinson, the house should have been painted several years ago. The linoleum is cracked and the hardwood floors need refinishing. It's such a beautiful home, but it's run down."

"Work?" came the gruff response. "What about the appliances you've thrown out? They worked just fine. All this new paint and people running around at all hours. A body can't get a decent rest around here anymore. Are you crazy? I watch you. You work way too hard. What do you want to prove, anyway? You remind me of my baby Julia," he finished quietly. Then he thundered, "You've invaded my house and it's taken you days to talk with me! I know you heard me, right from the get go."

"Me not listening? How about you not talking? Get over yourself, bub."

Abby stepped back. She'd done it now. She added steel to her whisper. "Mr. Wilkinson, uh, has anyone told you that you've passed on?"

"Of course I know I'm dead. I figured it out long ago. Little puppy, you. What's your point?"

She cleared her throat. "Well, aren't you supposed to go to the light? Meet family that has already passed on? I heard you calling for Lydia. Asking about letters."

"So you *were* listening. Huh. Light? I didn't see any light, and Lydia wasn't there, either." His voice rose. "The letters have to be around here somewhere."

"Look, I'm sorry the changes here upset you, but I'd like to make the house my own. You can understand that, can't you?"

"I suppose so. Well, you have done a good job cleaning this place. It was a mess. Lydia would appreciate your work."

She decided he sounded wistful. "Thanks. Now, how can I help you move on?"

"Play more Sinatra, and Big Band music. That stuff you call music gives me a headache."

"Oookkay."

"Doris Day. Lydia always enjoyed Doris Day. It'd be good to hear the old music here again. The good music," he added.

"I can do that, but the letters are the reason you're still here, right?"

No answer.

"Mr. Wilkinson? Didn't you want to tell me something? About some letters?"

The smell of tobacco vanished.

"Mr. Wilkinson?"

Chapter Eight

"I'd like you to call me Abby. No one has ever called me that. My mother always insisted I use Abigail and I—"

"And you never rocked the mom boat, right?"

"Right. But now I recognize placating my mom to make her happy has made me miserable. It's time for me to live in a new way. Using a nickname may seem like small stuff to you, but thinking of myself as Abby rather than Abigail fits the changes I have in mind."

"No change is small stuff, and names hold a lot of power, positive or negative, Abby," Sally said. Uncorking the wine, she poured two glasses and raised hers in a toast. "Here's to shorter names and bright beginnings. To the evolving Abby."

They clinked glasses and drank.

"Okay you have a new name, now what will you do after you finish the house?" Sally gave her a long look. "If you want to tell me, that is. Don't mean to be nosy or anything." She buffed her nails against her skirt. "Perhaps you'll start a family? Children?"

"No, no family close by. I'm fine alone." She sipped her wine. "I've had this dream. Rich, that's my ex-husband, he always said I had 'pipe dreams.'" She shook herself. "Enough of that subject." Abby inhaled deeply.

"My big dream is to settle in a house that I've

renovated and support myself with my art. In a way, Rich was the catalyst to my move here and the work on my house. He said I had the ideas, but they wouldn't get done without him. I wanted to prove him wrong." Her shoulders slumped.

"Rich sounds like an A-one jackass. Sorry, but it needed saying."

"Don't apologize. You're right." Abby threw her shoulders back. "So, here I am in Blue Peak. I have enough money to renovate, at least the basics. If I'm careful, I can live without a job for two months. After that, I don't know. The art may or may not pay my way. You know how that goes." Her voice trailed off.

"You're well on the way to realizing the first half of your dream, don't surrender right before it's set to come true. What type of artist are you?"

"Oh, I mess with acrylics. Some oils." She changed the subject. "What's your dream, Sally? Are you a pipe dreamer like me?"

"Hell no, I make my dreams come true. Just like you do. Dreams only come out of a pipe when you don't work at them." She tapped a finger against her lips. "Although, if my son doesn't get on the stick soon, my most cherished dream won't be realized."

"What's that?"

"Grandbabies." Sally finished her wine and poured more. "Some of my old students would choke to hear me say that, but it's true. I love the smell of babies. Not the dirty diapers so much, but that's the parents' dilemma. Me, I'll just cuddle and spoil." She lifted her glass. "Say, I'd be happy to baby-sit for you when your man comes along. You do want children? I can see you as a loving mother. In fact, I think a man is already in the picture. You only need to accept his presence."

No way she wanted Sally fixing her up with any guy, not even her son, whoever he was. She preferred dark-headed guys to ginger tops, anyway. "You said you taught school? Where?"

"Blue Peak College. Women's Studies." She shook her finger under Abby's nose. "Now don't you say a word. I believe and taught that women have the right to live a full life, however they choose." She pointed to herself. "Kick butt single mom, college professor, now store owner. My dreams, the big ones, have all come true. Grandchildren, unfortunately, are outside my control." She frowned.

"Somehow I doubt that. Does your son live close by?"

Sally checked her watch. "Yes and he should be here by now. I think he's bringing a friend."

Abby rose. "No. Oh, hell no. You're not setting me up. I have my own dreams, work to do." She backed from the table. "I'm going. Right now." She reached for her purse.

"Relax and sit down. It's just a meal between friends. There's no wedding ring hidden in the dessert."

"Hey, anyone home?"

The masculine voice echoed down the hall and Abby's knees grew weak. She dropped into her chair. Oh, no. Not him. *Carlos* was Sally's son? Or was he the friend?

"Carlos, sweetie. In the kitchen." Sally smirked. "I have company, someone you'll want to see."

A soft swear word echoed down the hall. "Okay, but my plans changed. I can't stay long."

She'd bet his plans had altered that minute.

Sounded as if Carlos hated getting set up as much as she.

"I forgot I've got a date." He stopped in the doorway when he saw Abby. Then he moved to kiss Sally on the cheek. "Um, that is, I'm meeting a friend."

"You mean the friend you mentioned you might bring by tonight?"

"No, not her, I mean him." He winced.

Sally tilted her head. Her lips thinned.

"No one important." He shifted. "Anyway, it's just a movie. Sorry I forgot to tell you."

"If it's just a movie, why not invite Abby along? She's new to town and could use some friends her own age."

"No! That is, it's a guy flick. You know, excess violence, naked, um, women."

Abby's lips quirked. Finally, someone else sat on the hot seat. "I love action movies. Which one are you seeing? You wouldn't mind me joining you, would you? Or, I could sit a few aisles away."

Carlos blushed but on him it looked masculine. And cute. "Maybe some other time?"

"Have you eaten, sweetie? The meal is hot. I hate when you gobble down popcorn instead of real food."

He chewed a thumbnail. "I'll be late if I don't leave right now. Thanks anyway."

Carlos kissed Sally's cheek then moved to repeat the gesture with Abby. He stopped before making contact.

"Listen, I've gotta run. I just stopped by to tell you in person that I had a change of plans. You don't mind, do you? I mean, you've got company anyway."

"Go ahead. Abby and I are talking girl stuff. You

know, life dreams." She flicked her fingers. "Run along. We can catch up on your date tomorrow."

Carlos opened his mouth then closed it and turned. "See ya."

His steps echoed then the door clicked shut.

"You and Carlos have different last names?" Abby's face heated. "Not that it's my business, but I'd never have guessed you are related. He calls you Sally, not Mom."

"He calls me Sally in public, Mom in private." She shrugged. "Works for us, though I can't remember how that practice got started. I'm not much for titles.

"I kept my maiden name. Maybe my subconscious knew the marriage wouldn't last long." Sally sighed. "Carlos could double for his dad at the same age." She gulped her wine. "Now that I think on it, marriage to his father is the only dream I had that didn't come true. But then, I didn't work at it."

"Marriage isn't all it's cracked up to be."

"Hear, hear, sister. I could quote chapter and verse, but instead, let's eat."

Their conversation never regained the earlier ease level. After clearing the table, Sally only nodded when Abby said she planned working late. A lie, but after considering the matter, she knew another hour or two at the house would make a big difference. Even if her ghost interrupted wanting to talk.

She drove to Collective Unconscious. An extra-large with a triple shot would give her the energy she'd need. Head down, checking her project list as she entered, she plowed into a solid object.

"Oh, sorry, I—"

Carlos stood in front of her. He crossed his arms

over his chest, and nodded. "Abigail."

"Uh, Abby. I'm asking my friends to call me Abby, now."

"Abby." He rubbed his neck. "Look, if I'd known it was you having dinner with my mom I'd have changed my plans. You know that, right?"

She studied his face. "Sure."

"Carlos? Oh, here you are." A tall, thin, immaculately dressed and made-up blonde casually placed her hand through the crook left by his crossed arms. "I've been waiting for you in your office." Ignoring Abby, she tugged at him. "Hurry up, we don't have much time before the special screening of *South Pacific* starts."

"Right. Bye, Abby."

Abby placed her right fist against her stomach while her left hand pressed it in. Maybe that would keep her from throwing up on the spot. She'd really screwed up this time. She'd thought he was as attracted to her as she to him. Stupid. He liked sophisticated women, similar to Rich and his new wife. When would she learn? As far as she could tell, Carlos would rather she didn't exist.

****

"Jillian, I was having a conversation back there."

She huffed but kept her arm linked with his. "You were? Really? I didn't notice anyone important."

He gave her a sideways glance, noting her tight jaw and determined smile. He'd seen that facial expression before. His mind churned with thoughts that were almost too incredulous to examine further. Jealous? After three, or was it four dates? He'd thought Jillian understood the score. The dates were a good time, nothing more.

She pulled on his arm. "Carlos, the movie will start soon."

Carlos jerked his attention back to his date. Jillian reminded him of Sierra in a bad way, a woman unable to compromise at any level. He'd abandoned a career he loved over Sierra. Left his friends behind. Now Jillian looked to control him and his coffee house customers. Another mistake in the making, but this one he could rectify by clarifying expectations.

He needed to call some of his old friends at the college. Time he had his head examined.

Chapter Nine

Abby balanced the coffee and her purse in one hand while reaching for the lights. The overhead fixture lit before she'd flipped the switch. Looking down at her hand, then at the switch still an inch away she shook her head. Mr. Wilkinson, playing games. She turned away and the light flipped off then came back on again.

"Mr. Wilkinson? Are you here?" He'd better be or she'd get the hell out. The hour wasn't late but anything could happen after dark. Especially in this house.

The light remained on, its incandescence steady. She breathed a sigh of relief just as a door clicked shut. She twisted around but saw no movement. "Mr. Wilkinson?"

Pacing sounded above her head. Muscles tensed and urged her to flee. Abby called out again. "Mr. Wilkinson? Anybody here?"

His voice sounded from right beside her. "Ha! About time you came back."

She jumped. "Are you ready to tell me what's going on?"

"It's not that easy you puppy. Everything is simple for you kids. We were taught to respect our elders and to keep our troubles to ourselves. All that talk show garbage." His voice lowered. "I don't know what happened to people. The world. It all changed when I stopped paying attention."

Her anger slipped away, replaced with a grudging respect. "How can I help?"

"I don't know. Lydia wrote letters for—I have to find Lydia." His voice faded to nothing on his last words.

Abby sipped her cooling drink. Of course.

Another man who didn't want her.

She flipped the light switch off, locked up and went home.

****

Carlos stared after Abby. She'd barely looked at him when she'd ordered her morning coffee. No wonder after the scene with Jillian last night. Plus, he'd told her and his mom he had to hurry to make the "man's" movie, but Abby had run into him leaving with Jillian thirty minutes later. He could have stayed and shared a bite to eat, except the sight of Abby laughing with his mom had thrown him. She'd looked so right in his mom's kitchen.

Even giving her his best smile today couldn't make up for what looked like a heinous lie. He didn't blame her for ignoring him. Although he could've shown too many teeth. He'd probably looked like the Big Bad Wolf. Yeah, especially after sleeping late and not shaving this morning.

Well, that was all her fault. He'd tossed and turned, trying to figure a way to apologize. His thoughts whirled while his hands made change.

She'd seen him with another woman. He looked rough today. Didn't take a psych major to connect the dots. Abby acted jealous, but envy looked good on her as opposed to Jillian.

He'd escaped Jillian's clutches once again. She had

pouted when he'd left her with a good night kiss and nothing more. She'd shown her cards and it wasn't a game he wanted to play. Not after seeing the hurt on Abby's face last night.

Abby held his interest. More than any woman he'd met since Sierra. He'd let Jillian down easy while giving Abby time to get settled in town.

But he'd seen other guys sniffing around her and it twisted his guts. Not that she noticed them any more than she did him. He'd have to find a way to worm his way into her graces, make himself necessary to her, and he'd be set.

So what turned Abby on? All she cared about was completing her house. He snapped his fingers. Of course. He grinned and greeted his next customer.

****

Thump!

Abby stilled. What the heck? What fell? She moved from room to room, but found nothing wrong.

Crack!

The noise came from outside. She checked a window then grabbed the sash. Carlos stood in her yard, shirtless, his back covered with a fine sheen of perspiration. His muscles bunched as he wrestled with a stubborn branch. Wow. The guy hid some serious junk under his vintage shirts and pun-decorated aprons.

"I can't go there. Don't want to go there." And she knew exactly what "there" she meant.

Rubbing her hand over her mouth, she wiped her drool. "Wonder how long he's been here without telling me?" Her temper stirred. "Jerk-face didn't even ask if I wanted his help."

Yep, another Rich. Trying to take over my project.

Well, screw that.

Abby stomped to the door and out. "Just what the hell are you doing?"

He gave the thick branch a hard yank and staggered backward two steps. Looking over his shoulder, he grinned. "Hello to you, too." He bent over and gathered an armful of dead wood.

Her mouth watered. He really did have the nicest muffins, um, build.

Carlos straightened. His lips quirked. "See something you like?"

He added his branches to a substantial pile near the curb. Turning, he walked back to her, standing close, so close she could inhale his scent of fresh soap mixed with warm, very male skin.

"I'm here to help." His pupils darkened. His glance fell to her lips. "Anyway you need."

She licked her lips. Their gazes tangled and she couldn't look away.

A horn blared from a passing car, breaking her thrall. He didn't step back so she did. She jammed her fists on her hips. "I didn't ask for your help and I'm not someone you fit in between other activities. You seem to be pretty busy considering what I saw last night."

Crap. She hadn't meant to sound jealous. Jealous?

He closed the distance between them. "Are you sure you don't want my help?" He gestured toward the work he'd completed. "Besides, this is my apology."

"Apology? For what?"

"For last night. I hadn't realized what a bitch Jillian is." He ran his thumb over her eyebrow. "No one has the right to dismiss you."

Her stomach muscles clenched. "You know, I

74

wonder why you're taking on an apology for someone you say is a bitch. Makes me think you're playing the odds."

"I'm apologizing to the person I do like. A lot. Because she deserves respect."

Her breath caught. Rich had sounded just this gentle at first. He said he cared about how badly her mother had treated her. He wanted to make up for the suffering. Until he'd added to the mix before leaving.

Abby backed away from Carlos, his scent, and maleness. "I don't want your apology and I don't want—" She stopped before adding another lie to the discussion. She turned. "If you respect me, you'll leave."

He stopped her, his hands clamped onto her arms. "All I want is a chance to help you."

Her chin dropped. Yeah, right. Poor Abby can't do anything on her own. "No thanks."

"Fine." He released her arms then his finger lifted her chin. "Folks here lend a hand, remember? It's a way of life in Blue Peak. If that lifestyle doesn't suit you, maybe you should leave. Go back to Charlotte and hide."

Carlos walked away, snatching his shirt off the newly trimmed lilac bush on his way. He didn't look back.

Her throat closed. She'd invested everything, her money and hopes, into this house. So she was a little slow meeting people. She hired local contractors, and wasn't that helping the Blue Peak economy? Wasn't that good enough?

Would she ever find a place she fit?

****

"Hey girlfriend, come out here. I need help."

Abby dropped what she was doing and ran to the front door. Her neighbor stood on the porch with a covered plate that emanated warm and wonderful smells.

"My special muffins." She pushed the plate at Abby. "I don't have much time, I've got to get to the store. Eat one right now. You are too skinny, girl."

Abby laughed. "Yes, Mom." She lifted the plate to her face, inhaling the sweet scent of warm raisins. "Yum. Thanks for the treats."

Sally perched on her tall heels like a stilt walker. "I forgot to tell you how glad I am that you had Carlos trim the bushes yesterday. I could barely see around them when I pulled out of my drive. I didn't want to say anything given your workload. You made a good move, asking for help. You're fitting right in here."

She turned on her heels, running lightly down the stairs. She looked over her shoulder as she walked. "He'll take care of the grass for you, too."

Sally slid behind the wheel. "See ya later." In the flick of a fake eyelash she'd backed out the drive and disappeared around the corner.

Abby closed her mouth before flies could lay eggs. She sank onto the top step.

Her glance scanned the yard. She'd been too irate to really look, to give Carlos his due. Dried limbs and brush were neatly stacked a short distance from the street, just far enough back that they weren't a safety hazard to drivers. Her head dropped forward onto her palm as she groaned. She was an ass and she had some serious apologizing to do.

She'd call right now. Straightening her shoulders,

she moved into the house. Time she faced up to her difficulties, including pushing her reluctant ghost for answers.

Abby's stomach churned as she reached for her phone. Enough of acting the idiot. Decide what to say and dial the damn phone. If he's there, he's there. If he's not...she'd call back later. She held the phone in a tight grip, concentrated on hitting the right numbers as printed on her to-go cup. Carlos answered after a moment.

"Hi." She cringed. Her voice sounded like the Chipmunks on amphetamines. Quickly clearing her throat she repeated, "Hi, Carlos. It's Abby."

No response. Could anything be worse than dead air at the start of an apology? Her frozen brain refused to provide an answer.

"Hello? Carlos?"

His voice, cool, calm, and impersonal, replied, "Abby."

Her stomach stopped churning and hit the spin cycle. "I called to apologize."

More dead air greeted her announcement. Had she been cut off?

"Apology? Why?"

Carlos sounded distant. Oh, that's right, the phone needed to be next to her ear to work best. She shook her head, replaced the receiver and gulped a breath.

"Yes. I'm sorry I bit your head off yesterday." She pushed another breath into her lungs. Her left hand cramped. She released her grip on the counter and shook out the kink.

"I lost my temper. Thanks for your help with the yard." There. She'd apologized.

"Apology accepted."

"Really?" Her feet tapped a happy dance.

"Really. So now you're up for people helping you, right?"

"Well, um, maybe." With restrictions. And if they followed her list. Maybe.

"Listen I've got to run. We just got a delivery."

"Sure, okay. Thanks again and I hope we can be friends."

"We'll talk later, okay? Bye."

Too easy. Her mother would have made her grovel longer.

****

Carlos looked at the phone in his hand as if it were a cockroach in his kitchen. He thrust it onto the counter and stood head down, hands on his hips.

Friends? Like hell. He didn't know what he wanted from Abby right this second, but he knew it wasn't friendship. He had casual friends and guys he worked out with. No, he wanted a lover. Scratch that, he wanted what Sierra hadn't been able to give. Well, not give to him anyway. Maybe Abby would fit the bill, maybe she wouldn't.

He had a bad feeling a romance with Abby wouldn't go smoothly. But then, he hadn't admitted to problems until Sierra walked. He'd suspected. A woman can only put off wedding plans so long until even the groom-to-be wondered. Okay, so he had selective vision.

He replayed Abby's apology. The words had come rushing out as if...as if she were afraid. He had to decide if he'd push her or wait. She'd agreed to assistance. How would she react to his next offensive?

Chapter Ten

"That's Amore" wafted from her media player's speakers. She leaned against the kitchen counter and lifted the lid on her to-go cup. The aroma wafting up jolted her memory. That short lapse when she'd thought Carlos had undressed her with his eyes earlier today had *not* happened. He's polite to his customers and that's all I am. A customer. A potential friend. He's certainly made that clear enough.

Damn, though, he's one fine looking man. Especially given his tousled appearance today. He aced the scruffy look. What'd it be like to date him? She caught her breath. Where was her brain? Not in her head, obviously. This infatuation was too dumb for words. A sudden infusion of tobacco aroma hit her nostrils.

"Coffee, what I wouldn't give to have just one sip. And that smells pretty good. Not as good as Lydia's, of course."

"Good morning, Mr. Wilkinson."

"Good morning. Say, what is your name, anyway? Never thought to ask. Abigail, isn't it? You sure do remind me of Julia, though."

"I'm Abby."

"Call me Gordon."

She wondered what he'd looked like alive. His voice was strong if a little raspy, his speech, direct.

"Nice to meet you, Gordon."

"Hmm, doubt that," he harrumphed.

"Can you tell me more about the letters, or am I too nosy?"

"You're in a hurry to know, aren't you? What's the matter, don't want me around? Lydia always said I was good company."

"Gordon, I just want to help."

"I appreciate that but I have to tell you, well, what I need to do is kind of touchy. I'm not really sure how to explain it to you."

"Fine. Take your time while I start on today's project." He'd sounded embarrassed. Too bad she couldn't see his face.

"What are you doing now? Why do you always work so hard?"

"I'm trying to save the kitchen cabinets," Abby answered quickly, ducking his second question. "I found some dry rot in the upper ones. May have to replace them."

"Hmph, excuses. I 'spose what's there isn't good enough. Well, we won't talk about that."

"Would you tell me about Lydia?" She held her breath.

After a short pause, he sighed. "Lydia was my life. We made a pact. Whoever died first would meet the other when it was their time. Lydia said that's how it works and I believed her. But she didn't show when I died. No one did. I'm stuck here."

She lightly scratched her head. "Sorry, I can't help you with that. I don't talk to ghosts all that much."

"No? Well, can't say as I blame you. We don't have much of a life. Ha, ha, ha. Get it? Much of a life."

Abby laughed aloud in spite of herself. She liked Gordon. Yikes. Job delays she could handle but hauntings? She'd never been driven crazy in quite this way by a renovation.

"You know, Lydia would love to see what you've done here. She was always after me to update but I hated change." He sighed. "And here I am, stuck in the biggest change life has to offer, and I don't know where to go."

Abby gave silent thanks for the opening. "Perhaps I can help you Gordon. I don't know much about the Other Side—"

"Hell, you don't know much about life, you puppy."

"But," she ignored his interruption, "I want to learn. I'll help you any way I can." She let out a breath she hadn't realized she'd held.

"You just want me gone from here. Why should I trust you? Never seen you before."

"Don't you want to move on?"

"Only if I'll meet Lydia. Otherwise, I'm happy right here."

"Great. Sorry, but I hadn't figured on living with a ghost."

"Can't say as I blame you, but I don't have many choices."

Abby focused on the cabinets. The only thing worse than an obstinate man was a stubborn male ghost.

****

Sally hopped onto a stool and planted her elbows on the counter. Carlos placed his hands palm down in front of her. "Hi. You want your regular?"

"What are you doing dating Jillian Colvin? She's

worse than Sierra. I hope you haven't been out together more than once. She's the jealous type."

Lightheaded, he leaned against the counter. "What have you heard about Jillian?"

"Honey, if you don't want to cause talk, take your dates to Asheville."

"I—"

She held her hand up, palm forward. "Don't tell me."

He admired her split-second timing when she spoke next.

"Of course, I'm here if you need a confessor."

He straightened. "Jillian knows I only want casual. We talked about it. That's all it's been. A movie or two. Dinner. Maybe we went hiking one afternoon."

Her look left him feeling five years old again.

He huffed. "Okay, so we went out more than once or twice. That doesn't mean an engagement."

"Those words from the man who never dates the same woman more than twice? Tell me you've been seeing her longer than two weeks. That number of dates, spread out over a period of time, not so bad. All in a row?" She shook her head.

He gulped. "Um, oh, shit."

"That's what I thought. You gave her hope and that's dangerous with a woman like her."

"I sat down with her earlier today and explained that I don't have time to date."

"That clarifies the word from the beauty salon. I heard Jillian drove away from here burning rubber."

He grimaced. "Look, I made a mistake. I apologized to her. What's the big deal?"

She looked about to light into him then huffed a

breath. "You know."

He raised his hands. "Okay, okay, I screwed up. Isn't that what you wanted to hear?"

She grinned. "That'll do for now. Wait. How about a glass of the peach tea you made this morning?"

"You always know when I make peach tea. How is that?" He rolled onto his heels, wiping his hands on a small towel. "Do you smell the peaches from your store? Or is it a Mom vibe?"

He served her and leaned against the counter.

Sally took a long drink. "Yummy. Just what I wanted today." She caught his gaze. "So what possessed you to do the yard work at Abby's? You know she's a control freak. Or did you come to terms with her? Wait, is Abby why you gave Jillian the heave-ho? I hope so."

Both. He grabbed a hand towel, wiping his hands to gain time. "Nothing possessed me. I just wanted to help her out. She's got a lot going on over there. Plus, I was sick of hearing you grumble about the traffic hazard. Even though you never complained about the overgrown bushes until after Abby moved in." He narrowed his eyes. "Don't think I didn't notice."

"Ah huh. The bushes weren't a problem in the winter."

He threw the towel down. "Just say what's on your mind."

"The question now is how can we help Abby? Without her getting hurt."

"How about by leaving her alone."

She huffed. "Well, I never."

He moved closer to her and lowered his voice. "I've got a plan, Scarlett O'Hara. Trust me."

****

Abby heard scrabbling then a quick bark sounded at her door. Her stomach tied in knots. Had to be Henry. And where Henry went—

She moved to the entrance. Henry stood outside, wearing a trail pack that sported interesting bulges in the pockets. Carlos wore a tool belt and an inquisitive expression.

She wiped her wet palms on her jeans. "Uh, hi."

"We walk by this way every night and figured we'd stop in case you needed help."

She stared at Carlos. Her brain had melted, must have, because rational thought escaped her. Mentally shaking herself, she pushed the screen door open. The door hinges squeaked.

"Ah, ha. I have just the cure for those hinges." He stooped over Henry, unzipped one of the pouches and pulled out a can of lubricant.

Abby caught her breath. Here he was, interfering again. "I have that task on my list. I hadn't gotten to it."

"Then I arrived at the right time." He wiggled his eyebrows. "Wanna see my superhero tee?"

She snorted.

Rising, he placed one large hand on her shoulder. "Look, I get that you can handle this project. I respect that. Henry and I enjoy helping out. Give us some chores and we'll stay out of your way."

Fat chance. As if she couldn't feel his heat encompassing her from a foot away.

"Hey, how about that second step? It seemed loose. Fixing it will only take a minute." He put down the can of lubricant and pulled his hammer from the tool belt. He gestured toward the yard with the tool. "Or I could trim more of the bushes. Henry gets bored hanging around the house all night. He needs something to do." He narrowed his eyes. "You did say you'd accept help. The phone call? Remember?"

She glanced down. Henry's brown eyes pleaded with her as if she held a big bone. She answered slowly. "I have a list."

Carlos tilted his head to the left, his eyes held a quizzical expression. Now that she knew the family tie, she recognized Sally in that pose.

She threw back her shoulders. "I use lists to track everything." Her fingers curled around the doorframe. "If you want to help, you and Henry," she glanced down with a smile for the dog, "will have to follow my lead. No haring off on your own like you have. Okay?"

Man and dog exchanged looks. Carlos turned to her. "Sure, we can do that. In fact, why don't you give us our own task list?"

She smiled. "Why don't we see how you two do tonight? I've got standards to uphold."

Carlos shrugged. "I'll get started on the stairs and trimming brush. Anything else you want us to handle?"

She'd been putting off cleaning up the paint flakes and detritus left behind by the pressure washing crew. That chore was way down her list but it'd keep him busy outside and out of sight. Sally and her other neighbors would appreciate the yard clean up, too.

After assigning the chores, she walked back inside. He'd accepted her apology but she wasn't sure she wanted him around. He couldn't be good for her sanity.

Chapter Eleven

"I think our plan is working, Henry." Carlos hunched next to the dog, speaking softly. "She didn't kick us out."

Henry trotted down the stairs, sitting at the bottom. "So what do you think, boy?"

He decided Henry wouldn't commit himself. Smart dog.

Carlos scooped the last shovelful of paint flakes into a plastic bag as the shadows lengthened. He stored the tools and knocked at the front door.

"So, Ms. Supervisor, do you want to check our work?"

She stood poised, uncertainty written on her face. "Sure."

He moved, allowing her to step out. Henry pushed past him for petting and sweet words. He wished she'd lavish him with attention like Henry. Great, now he envied his dog.

They walked companionably around the house's perimeter.

"Wow, this looks tons better. I didn't realize how much the exterior mess dragged me down. It'll be a pleasure to drive up tomorrow morning." She held out her hand. "Thanks for your help. I didn't expect it, but I appreciate your work."

He took her hand, squeezing it lightly as they

shook. "So Henry and I can return? We have your stamp of approval? Remember, satisfaction guaranteed." He gave her hand one final squeeze before releasing it.

Abby withdrew her hand from his grasp, moving back a half step. "Well I...sure, if you don't have anything better to do."

"Make up a list for us and we'll stop by after work."

She took another half step back. "A list?"

"Yep. Wouldn't want us haring off."

She studied his face. After a long moment she said, "I'll think about it. Thanks again." She knelt and disheveled Henry's fur, burying her face in his ruff. With one final pat she stood, turned, and started toward the door. She called "thanks again" over her shoulder as she entered the house.

"Good job, Henry. Let's go home."

****

"Harrumph."

Abby jumped as the gruff voice echoed in her head. *Gordon.* "You startled me. I didn't notice your tobacco."

"Don't always want to catch your attention right off. Your young man left?"

"He's not my young man, but yes, Carlos is gone."

"Watch out for him. He wants to get under your skirt."

"Then it's a good thing I wear overalls."

"Young women these days. Can't help 'em, can't talk to 'em."

"You know what? I'm sick of your grumbling."

"Don't push me, girlie. You said that hippie girl

knows the letters are in the house, right? You sure you haven't found a small wooden box? Locked?"

"You've been here watching my every move. What do you think?"

He sighed. "That's what I thought."

A puff of fragrant pipe tobacco smoke hit her nostrils. "Those letters are personal. About a family matter. When you discover the box you won't read them, will you?"

"Of course not. I'm not a snoop. I want to help you."

"You may not say that after you know the truth about me."

Abby's breath caught. Gordon sounded…morose was the only word that seemed to fit his tone. What could he have meant? A family affair in which he'd acted badly?

She considered the subject while storing tools in preparation to leaving. Sure, Blue Peak seemed like the perfect apple pie American small town. But wholesome could still hide secrets, and crime wasn't limited to youthful high jinx.

Maybe Gordon's family matter was nothing more than him taking Aunt Sarah's silver tea set when it had been promised to Cousin Josephine. He seemed like the kind of man who'd lived within narrow societal boundaries. Conscious of his duties to family, work, and community.

Although, he did have a run-away daughter. Sure, she'd waited to graduate high school first, but Julia hadn't returned. Not even for her parents' funerals. Something sure smelled off, there.

Speaking of a foul smell, she needed a shower. And

she needed to get a grip. If Gordon wanted to tell her his problems, he would. She had enough troubles of her own.

On the other hand, she could better help him if she had more facts to hand. She wasn't really snooping, was she?

She'd sleep on those questions. Maybe an answer would show with the dawn.

Abby struggled toward consciousness the next morning. She grabbed a pad and pencil to capture the design she'd dreamed, a portrayal of various flowers in a bouquet. Her sketch was less elaborate than the vision: a large scatter of roses, spun out to the corners of the room, petals scattered behind. Her drawing was a profusion of roses in all colors and degrees of openness, from buds to fully blown, at once colorful, restful and unique.

The dream image called. If she used this design on the kitchen floor, she'd be giving up a week or more, taking time from other important items on her project list. She knew her kitchen would be special, but only if she gave up her carefully drawn plans and schedule.

She'd consider the project. Maybe she should rethink making her artwork pay. Or perhaps she should make her second dream a reality in a different way.

****

"Good morning, Carlos, I'm here!"

The shrill greeting from across the room had his shoulders around his ears in a nanosecond. Damn and double damn.

Jillian. What the hell was she up to now? Acting like he'd never told her he wouldn't ask her out again.

Talk about selective vision. The cloying menace

had drawn a bead on him. He kept his head down pretending he hadn't heard her.

Her too-sweet perfume reached the counter before she did. "Carlos, honey, how are you today?" She placed her hand on his forearm.

He slid his arm away. "Fine, Jillian. What can I get for you?"

She leaned toward him. "How about an order of you. To go."

He'd told her he wasn't interested yesterday. Hadn't he? Every face in the room had turned their way. Although he wanted to set her straight, he wouldn't embarrass her in front of her friends and neighbors.

"That option's not on the menu. Anything else? A cup of coffee to go?"

Jillian lowered her voice and leaned closer. "We dated multiple times over ten straight days. I'm not someone you can just dump for no reason. Men beg to date me."

Holding her gaze, he also spoke in a quiet voice. "Then you need to call one of those men. I told you yesterday that I'm not in a position to date right now."

Her eyes glittered. "Too busy helping out a certain neighbor?"

His hands fisted. "Not a topic I'll address with you." He stepped back. "Let me give you an extra-large of your regular. On the house."

Carlos could hear the staccato of her nails tapping the counter over the coffee machine sounds. He chanced a quick glance. Two bright red spots dotted her cheeks. The color faded by the time he'd prepared her coffee. He set the to-go cup in front of her.

"I'm sorry if I hurt your feelings, Jillian."

"Sorry?" Her lips thinned. "You aren't very smart for a professor."

Jillian grasped the cup as if it were something dirty. Eyes narrowed, she took two steps toward the trashcan, positioned the cup over the container, and released her hold. Head up, shoulders back, she marched out. The door slammed behind her.

Carlos let out a shaky breath. Close call.

****

Abby exited through the kitchen's glass-paned door onto the patio. The floor men had come and worked their magic, now drying finish kept her out of all rooms but the kitchen. She should be pulling out the rotted cabinets, but sunshine, blue skies, and warm temperatures beckoned.

The patio bricks needed resetting where tree roots had dislodged individual blocks. Half dead rose bushes ringed the uneven pavement. She leaned against the house ignoring the reality. Instead, she imagined a small table holding a carafe of coffee and a good book. Healthy roses in full bloom subtly perfumed the air. Her muscles relaxed. She almost heard the bees.

Why sniff polyurethane when she could be out here? Forget that. Today she'd work outside and maybe look for a patio set at the used furniture store. She couldn't smell the roses but maybe she should take time to trim them.

Sometime later a faint noise caught Abby's ear. She leaned her rake up against the house and walked to the front. Sally peered in the door.

"Hello? I know you're in there, I see your truck."

She grinned seeing Sally jump when she answered. "You're wrong, I'm out here. I'm having fun raking up stuff. Want to see?" She led the way, kicking debris off the path. Sally's yards of multi-hued layered chiffon wouldn't last long if tangled with a stray branch.

"Girl, I'm sick of seeing you in those old clothes. We should go out so you can dress up. I don't know what I'd do if I couldn't style every day. Well, to each her own."

Abby couldn't stop the snort that exploded out of her. She looked over her shoulder, one eyebrow raised.

"What?"

"Nothing, nothing." Her idea of styling and Sally's wouldn't match in this lifetime. She set up a new lawn chair for Sally then dropped to the ground, sprawling against a nearby tree.

Sally surveyed the yard. "You've been on a tear back here, too. Gracious girl, when are you going to slow down and allow things to unfold? Or better, yet, get help?"

She ducked her head.

"Oh, I apologize. I didn't mean to scold."

"You're fine." She swallowed. "Rich always handled the landscaping, so I'd ignored the front yard. When Carlos did that work without asking, it really ticked me off. Reminded me of Rich taking over, you know?"

Sally's nod and silence encouraged her.

"I kept putting off the yard work because I really need to move into the house." Sally's questioning look made her reveal more. "My money supply is limited, and then I had to order replacement cabinets when I hadn't included them in my renovation budget. Until this place is up to code, I can't leave the apartment. But I still believe in this project. I can do this."

Sally studied her hands. "Do you miss your ex?"

"Rich? Not really, no. His expertise yes, but his attitude? Nuh, uh." She caught Sally's gaze. "You've helped me understand that I can do this on my own," she smiled, "or with the help of my friends. I'm still working on that second idea, but if you know a gardener, I could use a name. My knowledge base doesn't encompass this yard."

Sally reached for her hand. Giving it a small squeeze she said, "It's my pleasure." She grinned. "I'm not much of a gardener but I know people who know people."

"I can pay them. Well, a little."

"Don't even start." She leaned toward Abby. "I happen to know that Lydia had some special perennials and roses back here. The Garden Club will salivate. I'm sure they'll trade your plant cuttings for their time."

Sally shifted in the chair. "Speaking of trade, you can help me, if you have a few hours to spare on Saturday."

"Sally, I owe you—"

"Stop saying that. You owe me nothing. I keep telling you friends support each other." She shook her head. "I need a hand at the store. Usually the Solstice drumming circle occurs the night before, but this year it's Saturday afternoon. I'd like to attend and keep the store open. Would you mind covering?"

This she could do. "I'd love to. I had a part-time retail job in high school, and I may even remember how to use a cash register."

"Excellent. Come by on Friday and I'll give you a crash course."

"I will. I'd love to do something for you for a

change."

Sally's face assumed an innocent expression. "I stopped in at Collective Unconscious earlier today and saw Carlos. He's made his special peach tea. Have you had lunch, yet?"

Abby's arm muscles tensed. She cleared her throat. "No, I've been pretty busy here. Plus I brought food that'll go to waste if I don't eat it today."

"You ought to try Carlos, his tea, I mean." She spread her arms wide. "I know. We should meet for lunch tomorrow. Bring an extra set of clothes. You can shower at my house."

"Oh, I don't think—" Abby began, her thoughts searching for an excuse.

"Sure you do. You think way too much. You need to get out once in a while. Meet some new people. They won't bite. Don't bury yourself here."

She thought Sally's eyes held a glint of challenge. "I'm outside right now."

"Abby, Abby," Sally shook her head. "You keep forgetting you're going to live here. You've got time. Don't try to do everything all at once. Come on, have lunch with me."

"But I can't afford the time."

"You can't afford not to take time for yourself."

"I'll think about it." Abby's excuse sounded weak to her own ears.

"I won't take no for answer. Just come on by the store at about noon or so. I'll leave my house door unlocked for you." Sally levered herself out of the lawn chair and picked her way through brush piles toward her yard.

"But—"

Sally not taking no for an answer? What else was new?

Chapter Twelve

An hour later a woman of medium height with gray hair neatly pulled under a large brimmed hat stood at Sally's side in Abby's backyard. Tanned skin set off her brilliant blue eyes.

Sally placed one hand around her companion's shoulders and used the other to draw Abby closer. "Abby, this is Cordelia Johnson, an old friend of Lydia Wilkinson."

Abby smiled and hid her doubts as they shook hands. Would a seventy-ish woman be physically able to do the work back here? Even considering her strong handshake?

"Welcome to Blue Peak, Abby. Sally told me you want to restore the gardens. I know they don't look like much now, but Lydia had the most beautiful roses in town. She grew old varieties, even created hybrids. We were in the same Garden Club," she ended on one breath in her clear, strong voice.

"Delia is a Master Gardener." Sally beamed at her friend.

The older woman planted her hand on her hip. "That's why I'm here. Sally said that Carlos pruned the bushes in front." She shook her head. "You'd better send him to me for a refresher course."

Delia huffed, pointing her finger at Abby. "Don't even think about offering me money for helping you."

Abby's jaw clenched. She cast for a reply but didn't get any bites.

Delia continued firmly, "This is for Lydia."

"Uh, okay, we can talk about that later." She felt unbalanced. "Meanwhile, what can I get you? I'm afraid I don't have many garden tools."

"I've got all the tools I need. Don't worry about me, either. I'm stronger than I look. And I just love challenges. I know how Lydia had it, if you want to restore the gardens exactly as they were, starting with soil amendment. You buy the materials, I'll do the work."

Still reeling, Abby found her voice. "Restoration is what I want. Thank you. Just give me a list of what you'll need and I'll pick up everything." She swallowed dryly. "I'd like to hear more about Lydia and her gardens when you have time."

"I'd be pleased to tell you. She was a fine woman." She surveyed the yard. "Oh, I see you've made a start out here. Looks like I arrived just in time."

****

Abby's thoughts flew like peas rolling on one of her mother's gold-rimmed dinner plates the next morning. The house still smelled like polyurethane and she had trouble concentrating. Like spending time wondering how to decorate her breakfast nook walls instead of focusing on the cabinets she had to tear out.

Wallpaper? Framed photographs? No, she had it. Trompe l'oeil.

Her pry bar made quick work of the dry cabinet wood. She pulled off the doors and let her mind wander.

Roses, her design would feature roses on a trellis elegantly framing the interior of the set back. Inside the arched alcove, a fountain, grass, trees and birds would bring the outdoors into her home. She'd paint the nook's ceiling the same blue as the kitchen walls, but add delicate clouds.

She set down her tool and reached for a notebook. Her quick sketch included a trail of petals from the trellis to incorporate the floor design. She made a note to buy floor primer and paint when she left for the garden center later on. Even if she didn't have time to start the mural, she could prep the floor. Paint would be less costly than the cork flooring she had in mind, too.

The design appealed to her creative side and she itched to get started. Too bad she didn't have time right now. She'd make time later.

She focused on the kitchen and saw she'd finished tearing the last cabinet out while she'd daydreamed. Once the pieces were in the dumpster, she swept and mopped the wide pine floor boards. If she hurried, she could pick up the paint and put down a quick primer coat before lunch.

****

Tobacco aroma settled around Abby's head.

"Glad to see you paid attention."

Lost in the flow of work, she continued applying floor primer, giving his words scant attention. "What? What do you mean?"

"The floor design. You dreamed that, right?"

Her hand stilled. The image had come from Gordon? Good God. What next?

"You need to get out for a while."

The issue could not be glossed over. "How did you get into my dream the other night?"

"I'm not sure. There's a learning curve to this ghost

stuff, you know. Besides, the design is yours, I just suggested you consider alternative floors."

"Actually, I didn't know you had ghostie stuff to learn. Is that what happened when the kitchen sink overflowed? You had homework in mop dancing?"

"You caused that sink mess. I just tried to help."

She shook her head.

He made a throat clearing sound. "It's a good thing Delia got here before you destroyed the rose garden. Lydia would never have forgiven me if I'd let you demolish it."

Her eyes narrowed as she considered whether to let him change the subject. Then his words sank in and her temper rose. "Destroy it? Are you insane? Don't answer that. I'm the one talking with a ghost. The answer is obvious."

Laughter rang through Abby's head. "Go on, get out. Meet a friend for lunch. That little hippie girl next door is good for you."

"Will you finally leave me alone if I do?" Abby bit her lip. "Gordon? I didn't mean that. I do want to hear your story and help you with the letters."

After a long pause she heard, "I know. I'm just a crotchety old man. Ghost. Get out of here or I'll never leave you alone."

"Gee, you really know how to charm a girl."

Abby bit back a smile as peals of laughter filled her head then faded out. "Okay, okay. I'm leaving."

                              ****

Sally leaned forward with a knowing grin. "Abby, what would you like?"

Abby's glance darted toward Carlos behind the counter. *Carlos.* Her skin flushed. Hopefully, she hadn't said that aloud.

"Where's the blackboard with specials?" Damn. Busted in the act of scoping out her friend's son. Abby hoped she hadn't noticed. Sally couldn't let anything rest.

"Just tell Carlos what you want and he'll give it to you," Sally replied with an even tone.

"What's good for lunch?"

"Why don't you ask Carlos?" Sally said with a smile that would send a diabetic into insulin shock.

Abby shook her head to clear it and walked to the counter. She thought he looked especially hot in a tight black T-shirt that read *I'm the Muffin Man* and, from her vantage point, what seemed to be well-fitted jeans. Yep, the T-shirt didn't lie.

His face brightened as he gave her a quick scan. "Hi, Abby. Back for lunch?"

She wondered if she'd really seen him looking her over. No, probably not, but she was glad she'd showered and changed from her work clothes. "Yep. The coffee buzz I got here this morning died."

He smiled and her knees weakened for a moment. She knew he spoke but couldn't get past watching his full lips move. She had a sudden wish to have them pressed against her neck.

"Abby?"

His voice sounded faint, almost distant. She thought her voice croaked when she answered. "What?" She tried to clear her dry throat.

"I said would you like to order lunch?" His eyebrows winged together. "May I make you something?"

Her unruly mind said you can make *me* anytime.

She shook her head sideways to clear her thoughts and gain control.

"Nothing to eat? Coffee then?" He studied her with a puzzled look on his face.

She cleared her throat. He'd think her a space cadet. *Say something.*

"No, I mean, yes, I'd like a tuna wrap please, a large cup of Costa Rican if you have it, and um, maybe I'll have a muffin later." Her voice sounded raspy. Too much pollen in the air, maybe.

He grinned and she decided to push for a law against handsome men smiling in public places. He spoke and again, she couldn't hear a word. Oh boy, she swam in deep trouble.

Later that afternoon, Abby walked into Collective Unconscious for a quick caffeine fix. She scanned the room. The blonde she'd seen with Carlos sat front and center. It would be impossible to miss seeing her, either from the door or the counter. Hmm, so that's the way the wind blew.

Her good spirits dropped, scattered like sand kicked by a beach bully. Good thing she knew the blonde remained in the picture before her heart got dragged into the same old dark hole. Why did she torture herself with thoughts of dating Carlos?

She smiled at the blonde woman, who glared in return. Abby stepped back, pushed by the force of the other woman's anger. She swiveled on her heels, walking like an automaton to the counter. No way she would tangle with *her.*

****

Abby had looked really hot today. She'd deep-sixed the overalls and had filled out tight jeans and a sky blue Henley top.

Good thing Jillian hadn't been in the house for lunch. Her sharp glance would've picked up the once over he'd given Abby. He didn't want that nutso picking Abby apart.

But man, he couldn't help himself. Laying eyes on Abby soothed his soul in a way even Sierra hadn't. He was on his way to being a goner.

"Boss, we need more tuna salad. We just got three orders and we only have enough for one plate."

"I'm on it."

He walked into the kitchen and washed his hands before pulling on latex gloves and an apron proclaiming, "It's All Gouda." It figured he'd fall for a woman with more layers to her than the onion he peeled.

He'd been surprised when she'd asked him for cabinetmaker referrals, but pleased she hadn't gone to the big box store out at the interstate. She'd called his friend Joey at Sandman Wood before leaving the cafe. And he'd called Joey after she'd walked out, ensuring he made her project a priority.

Maybe he should feel guilty for interfering, but he wanted that happy smile part of her daily facial expressions. From what he could figure, she'd had a tough life. His calling in favors was just a way to help her get settled in town, right?

He'd do the same for any friend of his mother's. Right?

Carlos walked out from the kitchen and spotted a tense nonverbal interaction between Abby and Jillian. Shit. He should have known his attraction to Abby would be fertilizer for the grapevine. Now what?

Abby walked stiffly to the counter. He smiled. She didn't.

"I'd like an extra-large cup of today's coffee special to go, please."

He looked at her, his heartbeat stalled. Her face was pinched, white, and unsmiling. He turned away. Damn him as a fool for dating Jillian, who hunched at the center table like a vulture. What a screwed up mess.

Abby's tight, erect posture gave his spine fits. She threw several bills onto the counter. "Thanks, keep the change." She picked up her coffee. "Oh, and I appreciate your yard work."

"It's been my pleasure. You know Henry and I walk past—"

She interrupted him, her jaws barely moving. "Yes, and I enjoy seeing Henry. Listen, I don't really have anything else I need help with, so don't bother stopping by the house. Thanks anyway." Her voice cracked.

The heartbeat that had stalled earlier now disappeared along with his breath. "Abby, please tell me what's wrong." As if he didn't already know.

She leveled him a look of disdain mixed with incredulity, turned and walked for the door. He saw Jillian's smirk, but couldn't tell if Abby had noticed. He'd like to ban Jillian from his coffee house for life. Wouldn't that fertilize the grapevine?

Chapter Thirteen

Today, Abby's reflection could nab her a zombie role in a remake of *Night of the Living Dead.* This was why she shouldn't get involved in romance. Men brought heartache and destroyed her sleep cycle.

Besides exhaustion, Gordon had hidden her project list. She had less than ten days to finish this job. Her shoulder muscles tightened. She could work without the list-she knew the items by heart-but she missed having her paper security blanket. Maybe she needed a quick trip to the hardware store to help her regain her focus.

Delia parked and climbed from her car as Abby left the house.

"Hi, Delia. Want me to work with you in the yard? I could use a break."

"No offense, dear," she said, "but I'll get more done if I have free reign."

The older woman reached into her pocket. "Say, I found this old photo of Lydia and Gordon. Must be oh, thirty or more years old, but I thought you'd like to see the folks who built this house." She sighed. "We were so young then."

Her hand shook reaching for the picture. "Yes, I would like to see them. Thanks for thinking of me."

The photograph was a faded color print of a middle-aged couple standing arm-in-arm before the front door. Gordon stood quite a bit taller than Lydia.

He wore a suit, white shirt and tie. His light brown hair was cut short and neatly combed. His jaw was square and he'd remained a handsome man into later age.

Beside him, Lydia wore a simple straight-lined dress and heels. Atop her darker hair perched a small hat. She held a flower bouquet in one hand. Even faded, Abby could see Lydia had a mischievous look on her face.

The pair smiled into the camera without squinting. They looked committed. She rubbed her chest. "What a sweet picture."

"Yes, they were a devoted couple."

She handed the photo to Delia.

"No, go ahead and keep that one. I have others, pictures with the Wilkinsons, my husband and myself. We enjoyed our outings together."

"Thank you." She placed the photo into her top pocket.

Delia's face turned hopeful. "Say, I wondered if I could take some cuttings."

Abby gestured toward the yard with both arms open. "Take whatever you want. I don't know what I'd do without you."

Delia's hand covered Abby's. "The rest of the Garden Club is coming to help. Lydia was our president five years running. But don't worry. I'll keep them under control."

Abby knew she wasn't good with landscaping yet she had a deep desire to restore the gardens. Who better to do it than people who'd seen them in their prime?

"Delia, I don't know what to say. Thanks and please take what you'd like. The rest of your club members should, too. Lydia will be happy you're saving her garden."

"Now how would you know that? But you are one-hundred percent right young lady." The older woman made shooing motions with her hands. "Now scoot, go on, take your break. You look as if you need one."

She didn't know whether to laugh or cry; she left.

The aroma of candles, incense, and potpourri in Good Vibes filled Abby's senses. This had been a better destination choice than the hardware store. She wandered over to the reading area to wait until Sally had finished helping a customer. Leaning back against the couch she closed her eyes and sighed.

"Such a sigh." The couch cushions dipped when Sally dropped down beside her. "What's wrong? Trouble at the house? Or is it something else?"

She pulled herself forward. Both, but she was only ready to admit to the house issues. "Gordon hid my project list again. The original, and my copy. I didn't want to confront him. That's why I'm here."

"You came to the right place. How about a cup of tea? I'll be right back."

She closed her eyes as Sally moved off. The tinkling of fountains and wind chimes blended together, underscored with soft instrumentals. Her muscles relaxed as her consciousness drifted.

Mugs clinking together were her signal to open her eyes. The cushions dipped again as Sally sat.

She reached for a mug, inhaled the chamomile aroma and took a cautious sip. Perfect. Another sigh slipped out. "Thanks, Sally. This is exactly what I needed."

Sally patted her hand. "That's why I'm here, sweetie."

They sat companionably and silently for a few moments. She roused herself and without preamble said, "I'm not sure if I can be ready by the end of the month."

"That worries you why?"

"I budgeted for delays, but money is getting tight. It'd really help if I didn't have to pay an extra month's rent on my furnished apartment."

"No problem, you can stay with me."

Her relaxed muscles tensed in a nanosecond. "Sally, no. That's not what I meant. I'm not angling for a place to stay."

Sally's jaw tightened. Damn. She'd done it now. Even with the visual warning, she wasn't prepared for Sally's response.

"You belong in Blue Peak. I've offered to help, so has Carlos. You turn us down or limit us. What's with that? Are you afraid you can't give anything back? Are you convinced you don't deserve to have help? Or is it something else?"

How best to answer all that? "I don't know," slipped out in a small voice. Her next comment was stronger. "That's not true, you know, about my not accepting a hand. Delia Johnson is at the house with the Garden Club. And Carlos—"

Sally captured her hand lightly. "This is really about Carlos, isn't it?"

Damn Sally's intuition. She took a deep breath. "Yes, I guess it is."

"What happened? Did he do something without asking again?"

She shook her head. "Why is he helping me if he's dating that gorgeous blonde? It doesn't make sense. I mean it's just a matter of time before he tires of me."

Sally flipped her hand in a sharp dismissive gesture. "Carlos is not dating her." Her eyes narrowed, searching Abby's own. "And what makes you think he'll tire of you?"

She sat up straight, answering the first question, avoiding the second. "Oh, yes he is. A tall, thin, elegant blonde woman—I've seen them together more than once."

Sally sniffed. "Jillian Colvin? She's the only person in town who thinks they're dating seriously. He told me himself that he has no plans to see her again."

Her pulse jumped. "Really?"

"Really." She cocked her head in a listening attitude. "That's a mistake he's paying for as we speak." She shifted on the couch. "So are you going to answer my other question?"

Abby tried an innocent expression but Sally frowned. She looked down at her clasped hands. "Men get tired of me." Her voice faded. "I'm boring, I guess."

Sally's finger tipped her chin. "You've been hanging around with assholes. Or maybe they had their heads up their asses. I know asses figure in there somewhere."

She giggled.

Sally removed her finger from Abby's chin. "Now see, that's the right perspective to take. Laugh. Everything will turn out for the best. Trust me."

She smothered her giggles. "The last person who told me to trust them was a magazine salesman."

Sally's right eyebrow shot up. "Did you order?"

She shook her head.

"See? Believe in yourself rather than thinking

you're less important than others and your life will turn around. Money back guaranteed."

She nodded. With friends like Sally, everything would work out.

"And if you need to leave your temporary apartment and don't come to stay with me, I'll make your life next door a living hell."

She hiccupped. Her hand covered her mouth.

Sally frowned. "You should be afraid. I can be hell on high heels."

"I know."

****

"Trust me, we're good together. Everyone says so." Jillian's eyelashes fluttered.

Carlos gritted his teeth. Her perfume nauseated him, and the last fifteen minutes of convoluted conversation with her had pushed his patience to the limit. "Jillian, I thought you understood."

He'd used English, hadn't he? Damn, this woman almost made him rethink his position on capital punishment.

"But darling, I learned about that little waif you've taken under your wing. I decided that your sense of honor wouldn't let you help her while dating me. If you want to work with her, and by the way I understand she's a lesbian, it's fine with me." She smiled, angling her face to look up at him from under her eyelashes. "I'm sure you're looking for a real woman. And I am real," she purred as her long, acrylic fingernails reached toward him, "all over."

He sputtered and his face grew hot as he moved his hands out of her reach. *Waif? Lesbian? Abby?*

"Jillian, really I—"

His barista broke into their conversation. "Boss, come quick." Carlos jumped, the reprieve got his blood pumping.

"Karen has an issue in the kitchen. She needs your help, pronto." His barista gestured to the customers waiting at the counter. "I can't leave."

He looked over his shoulder and down at Jillian. "I don't know why you aren't hearing me. I'm not dating you. Period." He barely heard her reply as he rushed to the kitchen.

"Don't worry, darling, I know you'll change your mind."

Damn it. The woman likely wouldn't take "no way in hell" engraved in marble with her name and the date for an answer.

With the kitchen emergency solved, he checked the coffeehouse and noted Jillian's absence. His good luck was short-lived when a familiar figure walked in the door.

Sierra.

Here.

Now.

Looked like his day to face his demons one-by-one. Too bad they were also back-to-back.

He moved to the counter in what felt like slow motion. "Sierra. What brings you here? An espresso, or perhaps a cappuccino?"

She brushed hair behind her right ear in a gesture he knew betrayed her nervousness. What did she have to fear? She had the life she'd told him she wanted.

"Cappuccino, please." She pulled out her wallet then met his gaze. "It's good to see you, Carlos. That is, you look happy in your new life."

He'd be dammed if he'd say the same. Although, now that he took a closer look, he saw similar signs of the stress she'd worn at the end of their relationship. She remained beautiful though, and his pulse beat faster than it should.

"Thanks, Sierra. I'll get that drink for you right now." He waved off his barista, glad to have an excuse to move away from his ex-fiancée.

"That's a to-go cup, right?"

"No, I'd prefer a mug." She fiddled with her hair again. "I'll drink it here, unless you have an objection."

He shook his head. "Whatever the customer prefers."

She settled at the counter, and a moment later, he placed her drink before her.

"I've got some work in the kitchen, so you'll forgive me if I don't stay to chat."

She placed her hand on his arm. "Carlos, wait." She cleared her throat. "I have to, that is, I came to apologize. Well, partly to apologize."

Her familiar touch shook him. He crossed his arms shaking off her hand in the process. "You're sorry. I get that and it's been said. I'm sorry, too, but we've both moved on. No need to review the past."

"It's not the past I came here to discuss, Carlos." Her chest rose with a deep inhalation. "It's the future. Your future, specifically."

"You gave up the right to discuss my future long ago, Sierra. Cut line."

Her face reddened. "Fine. I've heard, everyone in the department has, that you've been mentoring psych students here."

"Does the dean have a problem with that? Last I

knew, giving free advice didn't require a doctorate."

"True. But teaching at the college level does."

His eyes narrowed. What did she infer? She sipped her drink then raised her gaze to his.

"The dean noticed that students you've mentored excel. The department has an opening with your name on it."

His heart skipped a beat. He stepped away and leaned against his back counter, hoping the move looked casual.

As much as he enjoyed running the coffee house, he loved teaching more. Except for one obvious obstacle. The woman sitting in front of him. Oh, and her psych professor husband.

"Why you? Why didn't the department head contact me if he's so interested in my return?"

"I think we both know the answer to that question." Her hands cupped the mug. She kept her attention on her drink. "Sam and I...we've split."

His hands tightened on the wood behind him, unsure of his response to the words he intuited were coming next.

"It's not just the department who wants you back, Carlos. I do, too."

Chapter Fourteen

Abby paced. A new lawn chair and a small plastic table sat in the middle of the re-laid brick patio. Not as nice as the set she'd been salivating over at the used furniture shop, but her selections would do for now.

Before she'd left Good Vibes that afternoon she'd invited Sally for a picnic dinner. Her friend should arrive any minute.

"I hope this wasn't a mistake. Sally's home is much nicer." Music echoed down the street, growing louder. "Too late now. She's here."

Sally rounded the house. She handed Abby a small beribboned basket and bottle of wine. "I know it's not an official housewarming," she said, "but you deserve gifts."

Abby investigated the basket.

"The candles have tea tree oil, geranium, and citronella, all natural insect repellents," Sally said.

"I won't say 'you shouldn't have,' let's just open the bottle and light the candles. Thank you. Thanks for everything."

"Come on," Sally rubbed her hands together. "I've been dying to see the house."

Abby's palms dampened though the humidity level was comfortable.

"Don't worry," Sally smirked. "I'll like you no matter how hideously you've trashed this house in your make-over."

Her back and shoulders were tight. She managed a weak smile and handed Sally a pair of fluffy socks. "Just in case the floor is tacky. Shouldn't be a problem, but the humidity kicked in right after the guys left. And remember, I haven't finished all the work, yet." She brushed her palms over her thighs.

"Wait, I'm putting on my poker face. Okay, ready to go," Sally said. She looked over the small foyer. "So far, so good. But I thought you were painting the walls black?"

She managed to squash her nervous giggle. "Let's go upstairs first. You can let me know if you think I should change my color plan."

Sally sounded puzzled as she asked, "It's your house, why would I do that?"

"Well, I appreciate your input." She hurried upstairs. Sally had a good point. Why did she always think other people were smarter? Abby's nerves vanished with her friend's genuine compliments and enthusiasms.

They walked downstairs and into the living room. The fading sun set the room alight. All the windows were open, birdsong drifted in, and neighbors walked past.

Sally threw her arms open and twirled. "This is marvelous. I can't wait to visit this fall when you use the fireplace." She halted. "Plus, this is a good color for you. People should always paint colors that make them look good at home, especially in the bedroom."

Abby hadn't considered that as criteria but it made sense. "Let's move on to the dining room." As they walked in, the chandelier's crystals moved gently.

"I love this room." Sally pointed toward the window. "This faces east, right? The prisms thrown by the chandelier will make this room dance."

Abby nodded. "That's what I thought, too. I haven't seen them, yet, I've been busy."

"Well set aside time," Sally said. "Sitting in this room for a few minutes every morning will make the work you've done worthwhile. Energize you."

The chandelier tinkled softly.

"Yes, Ma'am." Abby smiled. "Let's move to the kitchen, but I have to warn you—"

"I know," Sally interrupted, "it's not finished, yet." They turned toward the door with linked arms.

Abby inhaled deeply and lifted the plastic sheeting covering the door, about to share an intimate piece of her heart.

Sally stood still, her attention drawn to the breakfast nook. "When I asked what you painted you said you messed with acrylics and oils. You didn't say walls were your canvases."

"This is the first work I've done like this, although I've painted murals in the past. I had a dream the other night, and this is the start." She handed her sketchbook to Sally, her hand shaking. "This is the sketch for the floor. If the design is no good, I can always repaint."

Abby's, hands twisted together as Sally studied her sketch.

Sally's ferocious glare took Abby aback. "No good?"

Abby shuffled.

"Do you realize the quality of work in this house, including this 'unfinished' kitchen, is excellent? You ought to know. This is your business." Sally exhaled.

Abby's pulse slowed. "Yes, but I never really decorated the other houses. We just painted neutrals so we could flip the houses faster."

Sally squeezed then released Abby's hands and turned away. She studied the room then swung back. "Honey, you should rethink that. The work in this house, all the choices you've made, well, all I can say is that this place is already exquisite." Her lips twitched. "Even unfinished."

"Really?"

"There are women in the area who'd climb over each other to have you decorate for them. And they have the money to pay and pay well."

Abby hesitated, took and held a deep breath. "I had hoped to make money with my art."

Sally caught the glance and returned a verbal ball. "I haven't seen your canvases, but if this house is any indication, you'll make that dream come true. And I," Sally linked arms with her, "will make sure you use your talent. Now, all this walking and talking has made me hungry. What do you have to eat?"

****

Gordon's voice sounded. "Your boyfriend stopped by earlier. I saw him outside."

Abby jumped. "Boyfriend? I'm a little old for a boyfriend, don't you think? And besides that, I don't have a man in my life." It'd be nice at some point, but not now. And not Carlos.

"It was that guy with the dog. He's sweet on you."

She finished packing up the food and stored it in her cooler. "Gordon, you need glasses. Oh, sorry, I forgot you've got no physical means to…never mind."

"I can see just fine, and that young man is sweet on

you. I know the signs."

She picked up the dirty wine glasses. "It's nice of you to say so, but I don't agree."

Gordon snorted. "He came to visit you but the hippie girl was here."

Abby put the glasses down and leaned against the sink. Against her better judgment she asked, "What makes you think he wanted to see me? He and Henry walk this way every evening. Besides, the hippie girl is his mother. You must know who Carlos is, he lived next door."

"No, she moved in a couple of years ago, alone. Lydia was ill then." He made a throat clearing noise. "Don't try to change the subject."

"I wouldn't dare."

"Carlos stopped in front of the house and looked around. Then he walked back and forth a few times. After that he kicked at the brush pile twice or maybe three times." Gordon chuckled, a dry raspy sound. "Yep, he wanted to see you and he wasn't happy you had company."

Abby smiled to herself. Maybe Carlos did like her after all. They could be friends again.

Reality hit with memory of the blonde-haired Jillian. She pushed a fist against her stomach. "He's got a girlfriend."

Gordon's answer sounded like an old shoe scuffing the floor. "That's not what I heard."

She straightened, stepping away from the sink. "Uh, excuse me? May I remind you that you told me you don't get around much anymore? Since when do you have a social life?"

He huffed. "I may be stuck on this property, but I

have visitors now and again."

She clenched her fists. "So now I'm a topic at Spook Central?"

"I don't know about that, but I heard Delia and the Garden Club talking earlier today. Say, they're doing a great job with the garden. Lydia would be mighty pleased to see the gardens restored."

She unclenched her fists and took a deep breath. "You'd better tell me the gossip you heard."

"Well now, let's see. You know men don't gossip, but I'll do my best to repeat what I heard from the girls."

She bit back the multiple rejoinders that came to mind with both the referrals to "girls" and that men didn't gossip. Although the "girls," were lively women for their ages, all of them had a young outlook.

"I'd appreciate that, Gordon."

"Delia said Carlos had been coming over to help you with the work. Then one of the ladies said everyone in town already knew that and didn't she have anything new.

"Someone else said she'd heard Jillian Colvin had burned rubber pulling away from the coffee house when Carlos told her he'd made a mistake by dating her."

She shook her head. Carlos had said *what*?

"Then Delia said she'd heard he hadn't really told Jillian she was a mistake. That was malicious gossip, and she knew for a fact Carlos was much nicer than that story made him out."

This was way more information than she wanted.

"So then Delia said she bet Carlos wasn't interested in Jillian. He wants to date you."

She was sorry she'd asked. This string of gossip

was too convoluted for a tired brain.

"See, that's why he came over to see you tonight. He's sweet on you."

Abby had difficulty following his reasoning but Sally had been right. Jillian wasn't his girlfriend. A grin stole across her face.

****

Abby ran into the store, laid her soaked umbrella down on a mat, and removed her raincoat. "I hope this weather doesn't keep people away from your event tomorrow." She gave Sally a damp hug.

Sally pulled her further into the store. "The Solstice drum circle happens rain or shine. However, I have it on good authority that the rain will stop tonight."

"Wonderful news." She didn't ask for the "good authority's" identity. She really didn't want to know the answer.

"Hey, Sally, I need help with a gift."

"What did you have in mind?" Sally steered them toward the counter.

"I'd like to give Delia something as a thank you for her hard work."

"Oh, Abby girl, the work isn't hard when it's a labor of love."

She answered through pursed lips. "She won't take money. I have to give her something."

Abby relaxed when Sally nodded.

"I'll help you, but not because Delia wants payment of any kind." She sighed. "I still have hopes you'll come around." They walked to a jewelry display. "I know Delia has a bit of arthritis. These bracelets have copper strands, just the thing to help her feel better."

119

Abby fingered the delicately woven piece. "Perfect. I think she'll love it." *And I'll feel better having given something in return.*

"Good. You can ring yourself up for practice."

"Bring on the register."

****

Carlos peered through the rain-flecked window. The dismal day matched his thoughts. He'd screwed up by asking Jillian out two weeks ago. A few dates—not even any sex—and his life turned to shit. Even worse, Sierra was back and he had decisions to make. He'd give his right nut to rejoin the faculty, but Sierra?

He recalled her auburn hair shining under the Collective Unconscious lights, her scent, reminiscent of vanilla, and her killer body that, if anything, was more fit than when they'd been together. Sure, his heart had taken a hit yesterday. He'd thought he'd moved on, but maybe he'd been fooling himself. Or perhaps he'd been surprised and nothing more.

Making a life's decision wasn't on his agenda today, but he'd have to consider his future, and whether he wanted to make another go with Sierra, soon.

His barista called. "Hey, Carlos, phone for you." She covered the receiver. "A woman."

Crap. He hoped it wasn't Jillian. Or Sierra for that matter.

"Carlos, I need you here."

The whisper hissed. He pressed the phone tighter against his ear.

"Did you hear me? Abby's over here."

"Mom?"

"Who did you think it was, Jillian? Can you get away? And bring us some muffins and coffee."

He couldn't focus. "Why are you whispering?"

Exasperation dripped from every syllable. "Because Abby is here. I want to surprise her."

"Ah, do you think that's a good idea? You don't know—"

"Of course I know. Just get over here." The connection ended with a click.

Carlos filled a box with bakery, a thermos with coffee, and a plastic bag with both. He shrugged into his raincoat, his stride covering the distance to the door in a blink.

Door chimes sounded as he walked into Good Vibes. Sensuous aromas wrapped around him as always in this store. Abby and Sally huddled around the cash register.

Sally waved. "A customer, and just in time to help train Abby."

He held the bag up. "I brought reinforcements."

His peripheral vision caught Abby inching back from the counter. She didn't want to see him. Why the hell had Mom summoned? In the pouring rain, no less.

"Oh, goodie." Sally's glee turned into a frown. "You better have a chocolate chip muffin in that bag or watch out, mister."

He bowed. Catching Abby's eye he said, "Your every wish is my command."

Sally huffed. "Yes, but you didn't answer my question. Chocolate or no chocolate?"

He smiled at Abby. "Chocolate. My favorite…too."

"I'll find plates and napkins," Sally said. "Carlos, are you staying?"

His eyes on Abby, he said, "Sure. The thermos has Kona."

Sally patted Abby on the arm as she walked past. "Oh, good coffee pick. Thanks, sweetie."

The wide-eyed look Abby sent over her shoulder didn't reassure him. Now that he was here, he didn't know how to begin or what to say. The truth, he guessed.

"Abby, I—"

"Carlos, I want—"

Their simultaneous words surprised them into silence. He jumped into the void.

"Should we flip a coin to see who goes first?"

A tentative smile flitted across her lips. "I will. I apologize for being rude the other evening." She fixed her gaze on the floor. "I thought you were going behind my back again."

His forehead wrinkled, and his shoulders rose toward his ears. Ah, hell, he may as well tell her everything. Well, maybe not everything. And maybe not right now. She wouldn't be happy if she knew he'd been calling in favors.

He relaxed his muscles, leaned against the counter, and lowered his voice. "I really want to tell you how sorry I am about Jillian's rudeness."

"You don't need to apologize for her. Again." Her left eyebrow rose. "Unless you've recently become her keeper?"

He kept a rein on his temper. She didn't understand but he'd make her see. "I'm apologizing because my actions led Jillian to expect more from me than I'm prepared to give her. She's taking her disappointment out on you."

"Oh."

Sally loudly cleared her throat, accompanied with a

rattle of mugs and footsteps. He stepped away from the counter. He'd completed his work here.

Sally bustled in holding a tray. "Sweetie thanks for bringing a rainy day treat. Let's sit down."

"Sorry, I need to get back."

Sally's forehead wrinkled. "Is everything all right?"

He hid his smile behind a cough. "Yes, I believe so."

"Well, that's fine then." She gave him a one armed hug. "You'd better not mess this up. I still want grandchildren and you're aging by the second," she whispered.

"Enjoy, ladies." Pulling on his coat, he gave them a small wave and left.

Sally walked to the seating area and set her tray down. "So did you and Carlos have a nice talk?"

Abby searched for a topic change when the door blew open. Whew. Saved by the door chimes. No one stood at the entrance.

Sally jumped up. "Spirit messenger!" She shut the door and looked out the window.

Abby blinked. She had a niggling feeling creeping up her spine. "What? Did Carlos not latch the door when he left?"

"He did." She turned, laughing. "Whenever the wind blows the door open, I listen for a message. The Universe is always giving us information if we'd only pay attention." She walked back to the couch and sat. "That was for you."

"F-for me? What is it?" Abby knew that this time she'd seen the curve for woo-woo land and taken the turn all on her own.

"Gordon hasn't left because you each have something to learn from the other."

"That's it?"

She shook her head. "Gordon will stay within the Earth plane until he completes a task."

"The letters."

"Yes, and he will speak with you about the letters once he comes to terms with his fear."

Abby had a feeling that she also had fears to face.

"Enough about Gordon. You have dreams and you are worthy of having all your dreams come true. Even those you haven't dreamed yet."

With these words, Abby's throat closed. Her chest ached.

"You'll face a crossroads. You must choose love rather than miring yourself in fear. Does this make sense to you?"

She nodded then shook her head from side to side. "Sort of."

Sally patted her hand. "You can choose to step forward into the unknown or to stay huddled in the dark. Lead with your heart and your dreams will come true."

Ah, motivation speech. She got that.

She grasped Abby's hand. "Trust yourself. You're stronger than you think."

Abby hoped she was right.

Thunder crashed and boomed late that evening. A loud crack of lightning followed immediately, pushing Abby's heart into overdrive. She panted, unsurprised to find herself upright, clutching her covers under her chin.

Wild shadows played on her mini-blinds and her

clock flashed. Power surge. She lay back down, her arm over her eyes and breathed deep.

Thunder and lightning continued in sound and fury as Abby tunneled under her covers unable to relax. Rain and strong winds pounded against her bedroom window. Abby thought she'd hate to be out in the storm.

This wasn't a fit night for man or beast.

Chapter Fifteen

Abby left her apartment early to check for thunderstorm damage at the house. Walking to the stairs, she saw an odd heap of dirty fuzz pushed against the door. She slowed her pace.

Without warning, the "heap" jumped onto four wobbly legs. A pink tongue appeared and short tail wagged. A dog? Friendly or not? Her heart beat faster. She knew to approach strange dogs with care. She stood still, afraid to move.

Sally appeared in the driveway, a vision in a gold silk dress. A thin gold band circled her forehead, and she wore an array of gold bangles. Her normal multiple necklaces had been replaced by silk scarves in complementary colors wrapped about her shoulders and throat. She resembled a human ray of sunshine.

She halted beside Abby. "Oh, it's your dog. The one I saw in your aura. What did you name him or her?"

Abby stepped away. "This is not my dog." The motley creature inched down the stairs and attempted licking her hand.

"Of course she's your dog. I saw her in your aura, remember?" Sally clucked. "She looks hungry, poor puppy. You should feed her."

Gordon chimed in. "Listen to the hippie girl. You need a dog around the place. A young woman alone should have a good watchdog."

Sally and her auras were bad enough. She didn't need Gordon's opinion.

"This is not my dog, and I won't feed her. Everyone knows if you feed a wild animal it'll come back."

Sally's forehead creased. "Isn't that the point?"

"This dog will be good for you," Gordon said.

Abby was thrown off stride by Sally's logic and Gordon's interference.

"This is not my dog." Her volume and tone inched up. "She must have gotten lost in the storm. I bet her real owners are frantic. I don't see a collar. Do you see a collar?"

She couldn't stop babbling. Not good. She didn't want more responsibility.

Sally bent to pat the dog's head. "What did you say her name is?"

She gulped for air. "I didn't. She doesn't have a collar, remember? Besides, you shouldn't pet strange dogs."

"You mean like you did when you met Henry?" Sally crooned to the dog.

"That was different. His owner was there." Abby's voice wobbled. "I can't name her; she's not mine. And I won't feed her, either. All I want to do is return her to her owner."

Sally remained quiet, soothing the little dog.

Gordon returned to the fray. "She's a cute little thing. Well-behaved. Won't take up much room. You should keep her. Dogs are good to have around. She won't eat a lot. And it wouldn't take much to fence in part of the back yard."

Another expense. She just couldn't do it, not until her business made a profit. "Isn't there a shelter in town?"

"No," Sally said.

"Then how will I find her real owner?" Abby twisted her hands. The last time she'd had a dog it hadn't ended well.

Gordon grumbled, "You don't need to find the owner. You're the one the dog has come here to help. She says her name is Bunny."

Great. Now Gordon was a ghost *and* a dog whisperer.

Sally straightened, wiping her palms together. "Take her to the store, we can ask around tomorrow."

Gordon's voice rumbled. "I don't know why you're not listening to me, you young puppy. Kids these days, they never pay attention."

She ignored Gordon's grumbling as her thoughts whirled. "We can't take her into the store in this mangy condition."

Sally tilted her head to one side. "You're right. We'll give her a quick bath, food and water at my house. You can't stall accepting your dog forever."

"Is it okay to touch her?"

Sally shook her head. Her lips pursed. "What do you think I've been doing?"

Abby knew Sally wanted to foist this dog on her for some odd reason. Gordon wouldn't let the issue rest either, and she knew he could stir up all kinds of mischief.

She wouldn't fall for that "no shelter" nonsense. Sally lied. She'd look for the shelter on Monday.

"Come on dog," Abby huffed, "Let's get cleaned

up."

"About time," Gordon said.

The dog followed her, acting like they had a long established routine.

****

Bunny led the way into Good Vibes as if she'd been there many times before, adding to Abby's unease. This had to be a lost local dog. The canine no longer looked like a pile of rags blown against the door. Instead, she'd been revealed as a medium-sized ginger-colored mixed breed with a poodle's curly fur and build. Her smile was friendly, her expressive eyes intelligent. She didn't look malnourished and behaved well.

"How could this dog show up on my porch? It doesn't make sense."

Sally raised her eyebrows. "The Universe has its own rationale. Relax."

"Relax," Abby huffed. "But my temporary apartment doesn't allow animals."

"You can leave her with me until you move. You should name her. Bunny. I think her name is Bunny."

That's what Gordon said. Abby's hope deflated. Maybe she should run from Blue Peak before she lost her remaining sanity.

"Moving away won't work," Sally answered Abby's unspoken thoughts. "You're here for a reason. Accept your fate."

"I don't know how to care for a dog." Abby's grandparents had given her a puppy. The first time the dog became sick in the car, her parents had given it away, even though she'd promised to clean up after the puppy. They'd never let her have another animal, and

Rich hadn't wanted to be tied down by one.

"Just show her love and feed her every day. Dogs are forgiving."

Once again she felt that events around her spiraled out of control. What had happened to her life? The next thing she knew she'd be dating Carlos. *Oh, crap.*

She exhaled through her nose, bent down and stared into Bunny's eyes. The dog tilted her head, her brown eyes pleading. She knew keeping the dog had moved closer to a done deal.

She gave the dog a tentative hug. "I give up. Okay, I'll keep her until we find her owners." She turned to look at Sally. "I should leave her at the house."

Sally shook her head. "No need, Bunny will be the Official Store Dog today." She whooped. "Whee! Solstice energy!"

****

Bunny growled. Her ears pinned back. Was that a special signal? Did the dog need to go out?

Abby couldn't believe this latest twist. A run-down house haunted with a ghost who didn't trust her, a psychic neighbor, Carlos, and now a dog. She must have done something really bad in a former life. Oh, man, she sounded more like Sally every day.

Bunny's body vibrated. Her eyes were fixed on something across the street. Curious, Abby tracked the direction of the dog's stare. She gulped.

If she had followed Bunny's fixation correctly, a tall man at the park's edge stood in her sights. That hair and those shoulders were familiar. No, it couldn't be. She drew a breath. Nope, plenty of guys had the same build. She shook her head and squinted to focus.

He'd never wear that shirt. She should know. She'd

130

returned plenty like them to the department store. He'd finally told her not to waste her time shopping for him.

"It's okay, Bunny. That can't be Rich."

Bunny didn't stir an inch, her glare ferocious even in a small fluffy dog.

"Bunny, relax."

Not sparing a glance at Abby, Bunny moved her back legs under her haunches and wiggled her butt. The dog appeared ready to spring.

Abby looked back at the man across the street. He turned his head. Rich.

After her initial disbelief faded, she headed for the door, ready to flip the lock and duck out of sight. A small group of laughing tourists burst in, expelling cheerful greetings on entering. Her body stiffened; she forced a smile.

She should have paid attention to Bunny's warning sooner. All she could hope for now was that Rich wouldn't notice the store. Right, like that was a worry. Rich avoided woo-woo stuff, along with green vegetables and sugar-free desserts.

With a last stare at her quarry, Bunny nosed around each person, unashamedly panhandling for caresses.

Abby was assisting a woman with candles when she heard a low canine snarl. She glanced over her shoulder and saw Rich standing outside the door. Crap. Maybe he'd leave without entering.

She returned to her customer just as the door chimes tinkled. No luck for her today.

A furry body running toward her flashed in the corner of her eye. Bunny crowded against her legs, ears back, feet in a wide-legged stance. She watched the door, plainly on guard duty.

The customer asked a question, Abby answered without thought, maneuvering her body to hide behind the other woman.

A high voice piped, "Oh look, Richie, what a sweet little store."

Richie? Abby flinched.

Yep. Her day officially sucked. Rich accompanied his new wife. Young, gorgeous, and cradling their baby in a colorful sling. She looked down, wondering why Bunny hadn't growled at the child bride. She certainly felt like snarling.

She sidled behind a bookshelf to watch the store's customers and her ex. Bunny slunk along with her.

He looked good, better than he ought. Not as good as Carlos, though. She checked her reactions. A molehill in her throat. Some knots in her stomach. Shaking hands. Well, maybe if she took a few deep breaths she'd be all right.

Abby sized up Rich's wife. What was her name? Brandi, that's right, spelled with an "i." She looked like an ex-cheerleader. Big boobs under the sling, probably big without the breast milk. Windswept, shiny blonde hair, a flat stomach months after giving birth, and long legs showcased in brief shorts. Hair color was the only characteristic they shared and even that was debatable. Abby hated her on sight just on principle.

"Richie, sweetie, here's that book I told you about. *Healthy Eating for the American Male.* You really should read it."

Abby stopped a snort in its tracks. Rich? The original meat and potatoes, "gotta have my beer, man" man?

His smooth voice caressed an answer. "Sure,

honey. Let's get it while we're here."

"Sure honey?" Maybe she'd moved into one of those parallel universes Sally had tried explaining. Either that or this guy was a doppelganger. She'd have Sally tell her about that stuff again.

A customer walked to the counter, ready to check out. Abby glanced at Bunny. The dog's lips were pulled back over her fangs. She considered putting her in the back room then decided Rich could take his chances with the pooch. If he were bitten, it was his own damn fault for walking into her town.

"You ready Bunny?" The dog shook herself. "Here we go. Watch my back."

She took a step, Bunny crowding her feet. "I said my back, not my feet," she hissed. The dog moved six inches away, keeping pace with her.

Abby swung up to the counter. "Ready to check out?" She worked the register in a daze, ignoring Rich, fighting to regain her composure. The transaction complete, she smiled. "Thanks for visiting."

She steadied her nerves with a deep yoga breath. There would be no getting around this. "Hi, welcome to Good Vibes. What a cute baby. May I help you find something?"

"Oh, what a sweet little pooch. Can I pet her?" Without waiting for an answer, Brandi knelt down, extending her hand to Bunny, then ran her hand over the dog's back. The traitorous canine moved closer to Brandi. Bitch. Abby decided the epitaph could be applied equally across the board.

"Abigail?"

She closed her eyes briefly. "Rich? What in the world are you doing in Blue Peak?" *And why couldn't you have been here last weekend, when I was home working and not in the store?*

"Came for the day. I wanted Brandi to see this town. You always talked about how pretty it is here. How're you doing?"

How much should she tell him? Might as well stake a claim. "Great. I live here now."

His eyes opened wide. "Good for you. You always wanted a house in a small town. Got a dog too, I see."

What? He'd actually listened to her? "She's a stray."

Brandi looked around, her hand still petting Bunny. "See, Richie? I told you it's better to adopt from the shelter." She turned to Abby. "I've been pining for a dog. I just love them. And this is just the cutest little bitty poodle mix." Brandi returned her attention to Bunny, who exposed her stomach.

Abby narrowed her eyes at the dog. She'd forget the expensive kibble she'd planned to buy, this dog would be lucky to get week old table scraps. Traitor.

Brandi's voice interrupted her internal rant. "You said this cute little thing is a stray? I'd just love to have her." She turned to her husband. "You promised me a dog, remember?"

The child bride had Rich and a baby, she better not try to take Bunny. "I'm keeping her." Well, that was one way to make a decision. Show off for your ex-husband and his new wife.

"Oh, pooh." The baby's legs twitched, its fingers stretched, followed by lips smacking together sleepily.

Rich extended a hand to Brandi. "Hon, we'd better get that book and anything else you want. Travis is waking up."

She stood with little assistance, using Rich's hand more for balance. "Yes, darling."

Abby walked to the counter, Bunny joining her. She forced a jovial tone. "Well then, let's get you checked out." Head down, her fingers were whirling dervishes on the register.

The family unit had almost reached the door when Rich stopped, whispered to Brandi, and walked back. She thought he looked a little sad and braced herself. She wasn't sure she wanted to witness what would come next.

"Abigail, it's great to see you." He paused then blurted, "You've put on some weight."

Something in her face must have alarmed him because he backtracked quickly. "No, that's a good thing. You look great. Happier. You look...like you belong here. I hope you have somebody special in your life."

Sudden tears burned for release. Sure, easy for him to say. He was all lovey-dovey with his new family. He could afford to be generous.

He lowered his voice. "I never understood what you needed from me." He paused. "It's not your fault we didn't click. You're a sweet person."

Her fingers grasped the counter's edge. This was so not the time for True Confessions.

He paused again, as if choosing his words. "I'm sorry I called you an emotional coward. If I'd been more aware then, I'd have known I saw myself reflected in you."

Either the world was ending or Rich's body had been usurped by an alien.

"I'm not saying we still wouldn't have split up, but

our life would have been different."

Her brain refused to work. She stood blinking, wondering when the planet had shifted on its axis.

He reached across the counter and grasped her hand. "I wish you all the best."

"Thanks, and good luck to you, too." Bunny leaned against her legs.

Brandi called out from the door. "Sweetie, the baby is awake."

Rich started for the door, turned back, shrugged and smiled. "I mean what I said." He held the door for Brandi.

He wrapped his arm around his family, ushering them down the street. Tears stood shimmering in her eyes. He'd turned her life around. Again.

Chapter Sixteen

Customers entering prevented her from closing up to have a good cry. Bunny stayed glued to her side, or rather her feet. She'd almost tripped over the mutt more than once. Fat lot of good her dog protection act did now. She'd rolled over fast enough for the beautiful Brandi.

Wasn't it just the other night that she'd thought she'd finished letting go of her hurt over Rich? The reality of it was a lot harder than she'd expected. If she didn't get out of here so she could scream, she'd scream.

Rich. Of all the picturesque mountain towns, he had to come to this one. Her bottom lip pushed out. He'd never wanted children with her. Or to travel to small towns for fun.

More people pushed into the store. Bunny pranced into the crowd, assured of instant popularity and garnering everyone's attention effortlessly. She worked her stuff, kids waiting quietly to pet her.

Bunny is accepted automatically. Rich pulls off the family scene. What's wrong with me?

Sally better get here soon. She couldn't take much more.

****

Bunny ran between her and the door. The message couldn't be clearer.

137

Abby grabbed Bunny's temporary rope leash and a plastic bag, flipped the sign to "Closed," and locked the door.

She stood unseeing outside the store, Bunny at her heels. Who'd have guessed Rich and his new family would show here, on the only Saturday she'd spent downtown?

A deep voice murmured near her ear. "I've heard of people unleashing their inner beast, but I didn't know you took the idea seriously."

Abby squelched her warm reaction. Carlos. Beast? Bunny. Great. She'd forgotten the dog.

Carlos stood outside the store accompanied by Henry. Bunny poked her head around Abby's legs, saw the larger dog and jumped to touch noses.

Carlos pointed to Bunny. "When did you get a dog?"

"This morning. She was at my house, pressed against the door like a pile of rags." She knelt and attached the rope to Bunny's collar, one of Henry's puppy collars left with Sally.

"What's her name?"

"Bunny."

Before Carlos could react she said, "Don't laugh. Sally picked it." Well, not really.

His lips curved up. "What would you have called her?"

"Gone." Bunny looked at Abby with a hurt expression. "Sorry, Bunny. I've never had a dog, or at least not for long, and I'm not sure how to treat one. I really don't have time for a pet, uh, animal companion."

He studied her. "What *do* you have time for?"

Abby wondered why he asked. She glanced at him,

but he showed only friendly interest. "There's a lot to do at the house."

"And after that's done?"

"Oh, a house is never done," she said.

"I need to get back," Carlos said. "You want to walk with us while Henry makes a deposit? That is why you closed the store, right? To give Bunny some air?"

"Yes, um, that's right."

Doggie mission accomplished, they returned to Good Vibes.

"How about I take Bunny with me? Henry could use the company. Don't worry," he said, "he's neutered."

"I don't know. She may not behave."

"She will, I can tell. I'd better carry her. Traffic is heavy today."

Carlos squatted and Bunny crawled onto his knees and snuggled against his chest. He held her close, and Abby sighed at the picture.

"Just come over after you finish here. I promise Henry and I will take good care of Bunny."

"I can see that," she said through a dry mouth. "I appreciate it. Bunny, you be a good girl and I'll see you later." Geez, now she talked to dogs. As Bunny left with Carlos, Abby saw her wriggle to look over Carlos's shoulder at her. She swore the little dog smiled and winked.

Sally strode in several hours later. "Time to close up, sweetie. Let's hit Collective Unconscious for a bit."

"Sorry. I need wine. A big-ass bottle. I'll share even though I'd rather drink it all."

"Where's Bunny?"

"Shoot. She's with Henry. We'll have to stop at the coffee house to pick her up."

They squeezed their way through the coffee house crowd. Carlos saw them a moment later, smiled and waved. "That smile is just for you, sweetie," Sally whispered into Abby's right ear.

"Stop pushing. I'm not giving you your grandkids."

"Huh." Sally gasped. "Oh, no."

Abby followed the direction of Sally's stare. A thin, auburn-haired woman stood at the counter smiling at Carlos. "Is there a problem?"

"Not if I have anything to say, no, no problem. Unexploded dynamite is all."

Chill bumps covered Abby's skin. She glanced over her shoulder. Jillian looked daggers her way. Her lungs heaved.

Carlos pointed toward his office. They wove through patrons and stood at the door, watching Bunny and Henry curled up, asleep on Henry's bed.

"It'd be a shame to wake them right away," Sally said. "Carlos, sweetie, would you bring us coffee and something sweet to eat? I need to put my feet up for a minute. In fact, you should join us." She grabbed Abby's hand and pulled her into a chair. "Right?"

Abby's energy flagged. Coffee and sugar wouldn't ease her sore heart but talking with Sally would. She'd rather Carlos didn't stay when he returned.

"You saw the mob out there. The place is hopping. I can't take a break, sorry."

"Your business doesn't include what I think it does, does it?"

Abby didn't attempt to follow their mysterious conversation.

He shot Abby a quick look. "Not now. I'll talk to you about it later. Be right back."

Carlos left and Sally leaned forward. She chatted about the drum circle until the coffee and scones arrived, and he left them alone.

"So what's happened? You look like someone's stolen your favorite quartz crystal."

"My ex, Rich. He, um, he came in the store today."

"Shoot. And?" Sally accompanied her question with a hug around Abby's shoulders. That's all it took for her story to burble out.

Sally hugged her. "Remember the Spirit message? You're stronger than you know."

"Maybe."

"No maybe. Sometimes you have to give to get." Sally pulled herself from the chair. "Now I'm off for home. Even with the sugar rush, I need sleep." She'd taken two steps when a quiet knock sounded.

Carlos stepped into the room. "Abby, do you have a minute? I have a quick question."

"Sure, Carlos."

Sally kissed his cheek. "Good night, sweetie. Call me. We have old business to discuss."

"I figured you'd wouldn't let me off the hook. Night, Mom."

He cleared his throat, his hands twisting a dishrag. "One of my favorite films is at the Second Chance Theater this week, and I thought you might like to see it with me." Before Abby could answer he rushed on. "*King of Hearts*, a French film."

Carlos asked her out? Carlos? She pressed her thumbnail into her fingers. Yes, she was awake.

He looked down and immediately stopped twisting

the towel. "But maybe you don't like French films? Subtitles?" He fixed his attention on her.

You love foreign films. What are you waiting for you silly girl? "No, that is yes, I do, I like foreign films. And the Indies."

Carlos's happy expression flowed over her. The room's temperature rose.

"Great, that's great. Would you like to go? With me? The film starts tomorrow."

Tomorrow looked way too close. "Oh, I don't know."

His disappointed grimace gave her a jolt. "Sorry, I wasn't clear. Of course I'd like to go with you. I'm just not sure about the day. Can I get back with you on that?"

"You bet. The film is here all week. You know where to find me." He paused, his gaze warming her further. "You should get home, you look dead on your feet, no offense meant."

"None taken."

He threw the towel down. "Henry and I will walk you to your car."

She spoke past a lump. "What about your customers?" And what if Jillian saw them together? She had no reserves left for a confrontation.

"It's quiet and I've got efficient employees. That's the perk of owning this place." Abby groaned at his pun. Carlos grinned. "We can slip out for a few minutes."

He whistled. Henry and Bunny stretched and shook themselves awake then trotted to their humans. They stepped outside and the dogs circled the area, noses to the ground investigating the myriad smells.

Dogs didn't have to date. They just posed, sniffed and knew. Too bad her olfactory senses weren't that sharp. It'd be embarrassing to sniff someone's butt, worse, she'd get committed or thrown in jail. Or both. Why couldn't humans have tails to wag at the least?

When they arrived at Abby's truck, Henry and Bunny touched noses again. Abby experienced a flicker of envy as Carlos lifted Bunny onto the passenger seat.

"Let me help you." He assisted her into the truck, softly shutting the door.

She looked at him through the window for a moment before lowering the glass. "Thanks." Her voice sounded husky to her ears.

"My pleasure," he whispered, his pursed lips catching her strict attention.

She bit her lower lip. Yep, definite trouble.

He rested one hand on the truck, his gaze on her mouth. "Please call me soon."

She chewed the inside of her mouth. Call? Oh, right, the movie. "Okay."

His gaze moved up to her eyes. She felt super glued to her seat. What had he said? She'd been too busy getting lost in his eyes. "What?"

The corners of his mouth tipped up. "I'd hate to miss seeing the movie with you."

"Right." She couldn't keep a conversation going to save the world. Why would he want to date her?

"You're tired. Would you like me to follow you home, make sure you get there okay?"

She shook her head.

"No?" He leaned against the truck. "You sure?"

She gulped, her gaze stuck in the vicinity of his lips. The way he'd mouthed "sure" had sidetracked her attention.

"Start your truck and get your heater going. You're shivering. You must be cold without a jacket." He slapped the side of the truck as he stepped back. "See you soon."

Her hands refused to move from the steering wheel. It was impossible to turn the ignition key with hands frozen at ten and two.

He smiled. "Go ahead. Henry and I will be gentlemen and stay to see you off."

She forced herself to start the truck. "Good night."

****

"We did it Henry, but I tell ya buddy, I could maim the sucker who came up with the idea of dating. Nobody can enjoy asking for a first date, it's frickin' impossible." Although Abby saying yes made him feel like a winner.

He thought back to her expression when he'd seen her outside Good Vibes earlier. She'd looked thousands of miles and as many years away when they'd met. Her expression had held a world of pain.

That's when he'd decided that as long as he was creating suppositions and caring for her dog, he should get something out of it. Like a date and the chance to taste those sweet pink lips of hers.

He ran his fingers through Henry's fur. He'd caught her quizzical gaze a few minutes ago, the one that had been glued to his lips. And she'd done that weird leaning thing that women sometimes did, the move that made them look boneless. In any other woman, he'd say she was interested in him. He wouldn't lay bets on Abby. Her wide eyes and inability to speak more than a few words only illustrated her exhaustion.

The telling factor would be whether she called him back for the movie. The call couldn't come too soon. If he'd gathered his nerve to ask her out only to get stiffed, he'd really be pissed. Actually, he'd be disappointed.

"Whadda ya think, boy?" Henry looked at him, his ears perked, head to the side. "Will Abby call me back?"

The dog's pink tongue slipped out of his mouth. His expression made Carlos think the dog considered the question.

"Never mind. Her actions are out of my hands." He rubbed his neck. "Come on, time to close up shop."

Chapter Seventeen

"Collective Unconscious Café." Carlos hoped this wasn't his mom. He'd been ducking her calls to discuss Sierra's presence yesterday. He couldn't talk about the situation until he'd figured out his direction.

"Hi, Carlos. This is Abby."

Her soft, hesitant voice sounded along the telephone wire.

"Hey, how're ya doin'?" He winced. Shit. He had to come up with something better than that or she'd bail on him. Carlos lowered his voice. "I'm really glad you called."

"Th-thanks."

Did her stammer indicate her nervousness? That'd be fine, right? "I hope you're calling to give me some good news."

"Good news?" She paused. "Oh, I hope so. I mean, if you still want me to go to the movie with you, I'd like that very much." Her voice trailed off.

He'd like to kick the butt of whoever had put such a hurting on her. He kept his voice low. "You bet I would. Have you decided on a night?" Soon, he hoped. The suspense gave him a sick stomach.

She began to speak, stopped, and started again. "Would tonight work? That's not too soon is it? If it is I can—"

He interrupted before she could talk herself out of

the date. "No, tonight would be great."

She cleared her throat. "Okay."

"Why not bring Bunny over here to stay with Henry? We can walk to the theater. And you can drive yourself here and home. That way you can come and go as you like. Or I can pick you up. Whichever you prefer."

He heard her deep sigh of relief. "Thank you for the choices." Silence descended along the line. "Would you like to see what I've done with the house? We can decide logistics from there."

Carlos bobbled the phone. "You bet. What time?"

They agreed and hung up.

He had about six hours to get his nerves under control. He pawed through his junk drawer for antacids. God, he hated dating.

****

Bunny strutted into Good Vibes.

"Well, look at you," Sally crooned. "What a good mommy you have. So fashion conscious with your new collar and matching bows."

Abby cringed. "Uh, Sally? Do you mind not calling me Bunny's mommy? No offense, Bunny."

"We have to teach your mommy about dog speak, don't we, Bunny?" Sally continued, "She's a fast learner, though, don't worry, it won't take long."

The dog's tongue lolled.

"I, uh, want to ask a favor." Her voice raised on the last word.

"Sure, anything."

"I don't want to lose my security deposit, so I wondered if you'd help with Bunny."

"You want me to keep her for you?"

"Actually, I'm thinking about moving in early. The house isn't complete, but I can work around boxes. I guess. The furniture store said they could deliver a bed and appliances day after tomorrow."

"Ask Carlos to keep Bunny. He's got a fenced yard and Henry will like the company."

"He'll think I'm being pushy."

"No, he won't. I taught him better than that."

"Well, if he says no, will you take Bunny? During the day?"

"Sure, and I'll help you move boxes. For that matter, so will Carlos. He can call some guys to help."

"I can get it."

"No, *we* can get it done. Just name the day," Sally said.

Abby hesitated. Would it really hurt to have some help?

"In fact, why don't you move everything at once? Save money on your storage unit."

"You're right, I guess." Why was it so hard to deviate from her plan?

"Store stuff in my garage if you like," Sally offered.

She forgot herself and thought aloud. "I need an inspection before I can live at the house."

"Leave that up to me." Sally wiggled her eyebrows. "I have friends of friends at City Hall."

She rubbed her chest. "Most of the painting is done, the floors are complete. I just have the kitchen work left, and that's cosmetic except for the appliances. How stringent are the city inspectors? Do you think they'll pass my house?"

"I know it. You've done way more than necessary

for occupancy. Stop worrying. You can prove you've purchased a stove and fridge, right?"

Abby nodded. She swallowed her doubts, excited her dream was coming true. Sure, it wasn't the way she'd wanted the move to happen, but nothing had gone according to plan since she'd relocated. "Let's do it."

"All right, it's a date," Sally said.

"Another one." Abby laughed and headed for the door with Bunny.

****

"It's about time you showed up around here."

Gordon sounded gruffer than usual. "I've been busy. Sally asked for help this weekend."

"I guess an old ghost doesn't matter."

Her temper rose. "It's not as if you've bothered telling me what's going on. Are you ready to talk about why you're still here?"

"Almost."

"Almost," she echoed.

He coughed. "You've got enough going on here, my little problem can wait."

"Oh no, you don't." Her mother was the Guilt Queen; this was old hat. "I'll help you, anytime, anyway I can. Don't you dare push your inability to tell your story off on me." Boy, saying that felt good.

"I'll think about it."

"I don't mind you here, but you can't stay forever." She tapped her foot. "Gordon? Did you hear me?"

No answer.

"Damn, I hate when he leaves without saying good-bye."

Chapter Eighteen

Carlos smoothed his damp palms over his slacks and knocked at Abby's screen door.

Abby walked toward him dressed in black slacks and an electric blue sleeveless blouse. Her hair fell loose around her shoulders. She wore simple gold jewelry and a light scent, something a little spicy, like cinnamon. His mouth watered.

"Hi." She opened the door, Bunny at her heels. "Where's Henry? Seems odd to see you at the door without him beside you."

"He's in the car. It's cool and the windows are down. I planned to park behind the coffee house and leave him in my office." He walked into a potpourri of construction smells.

"Watch out for the tarps and paint cans, I don't want you to trip. The painters showed up out of the blue today. Not that I'm complaining, but I didn't expect them until next week at the earliest."

"I know this place is a mess, but you've done so much work outside, I thought I'd give you a little tour." She caught his gaze. "As a thank you."

He kissed her cheek. Smooth skin. "Thanks." He petted Bunny. "Hey, cute thing."

"I have some bottled water in my cooler if you'd like a drink."

Carlos shook his head. "Nope. I'll take that tour

now. We need to leave pretty soon."

"The upstairs isn't complete, so I'll just show you my favorite rooms down here." A blush spread onto her neck.

They walked through the rooms, Abby talking about colors and work schedules. The passionate light playing across her face during her monologue entranced him.

"The kitchen really is a work in progress." Her hands stilled at her sides. "It's also my most personal room so far."

Warning noted. He plastered a careful smile on his face and ducked around plastic blocking the doorway. After a quick scan, his smile dropped, his mouth hung open. "Wow."

Abby's breakfast nook boasted a detailed garden scene sketch, partially painted. The floor sported a base coat and he held the plans in his hands. Both designs had a simplicity that masked an exquisite attention to detail and underlying coordination of purpose. Sitting at a table in her kitchen would be like enjoying a colorful garden, even in the winter. Without mosquitoes. Nice.

He wondered if she'd take a commission for a mural at Collective Unconscious. It'd be a great way to spend more time with her. He'd have to tell her about his maneuverings on her behalf first. Especially because he'd promised Abby he'd keep his hands off her project. It'd be just like Jillian to pass along gossip to Abby, although in his case, she'd be telling the truth about his actions.

He knew he should also mention Sierra, because chances were good she'd be at the theater. The film was also a favorite of hers. Even if she weren't there tonight, someone had to have recognized her and wondered why she'd come into the coffee house. All it'd take was Abby hearing about his ex-fiancée's return to put the kibosh on his plans. Jillian would love that.

He'd examined his reaction to seeing Sierra again and determined it'd been shock. They'd kept out of each other's ways since their split, remaining polite when they did run into each other, which hadn't been often. He'd never expected her to walk into his place. The thrill he'd once felt for Sierra had disappeared. But his need to teach had not. He had a serious decision to make.

Bunny clicked into the room. She butted her head against his calf then looked him square in the eyes. What was that all about? Shit, he'd forgotten the time. Checking his watch, he noticed they could settle the dogs and make the movie if they left immediately.

"I hate to say this, but we have to leave or we'll miss the film."

"Oh, right." She let out a breath. "Thanks for liking my work."

Damn it. Would she believe he'd been blown away? Not likely. Better to keep his mouth shut. And confess his sins later.

"Did you decide about driving?"

She blushed. "I thought I'd ride with you. You know, because you live so close, it'd be silly to take two vehicles."

He kept his hands at his sides and his grin under wraps when he wanted to break into a victory dance like a wide receiver after scoring a touchdown.

"That's perfect."

She looked flustered. Good, so was he.

They pulled up next to the coffee house's office entrance. Abby jumped from the car with Bunny right behind her before he could get around to help her out. His lips thinned. Either some guy from her past needed a serious lesson in manners or she'd gone into independent mode.

After settling the dogs they walked to the theater. Given the way other pedestrians craned their necks, gossip about them moved faster than an all-points bulletin. He'd really have to tell Abby about the actions he'd taken on her behalf. It wouldn't be long before someone would talk. Either about his machinations or Sierra.

"Carlos, would you do me a favor?"

"Sure."

"Tell me, do I have food on my face? Or are my clothes out of order?"

He slid his gaze slowly over her. "I don't see a thing wrong."

Abby licked her lips. "I feel as if I'm under a microscope or something."

"Oh you mean the curious looks?" He smiled. "It's a small town, Abby, everyone knows everybody's business."

With a boyish grin, he said, "Let's give them something to talk about."

He grasped her hand, their fingers entwined. Her hand was firm, dry, and she had calluses on her fingers. He felt a sense of rightness with her, one that remained as they viewed the film.

The night had a cool edge when they walked out of the theater. Abby shivered.

"Chilled?" Carlos asked. Without another word, he

released her hand and put his arm around her, drawing her close. She was the height and size he'd always preferred. Her body felt perfect nestled under his arm.

His groin muscles tensed. Kiss or no kiss? Now or later? Damn dating crap.

Light from the street lamp illuminated her face and his arm tightened fractionally. He slowed to a halt and turned her to face him, holding her in a light embrace. "You attracted me from the first moment. Something, your passion, your art, draws me to you."

"Another pun?"

"Unintended. This is no pun." He spanned the bottom half of her face with his fingers. "May I kiss you?" The whisper of a gentle exhalation gave him permission. He didn't care if it was a breath or a yes. He was going in.

He'd planned a gentle, quick exploration of her lips. Damned reality threw him. Soft skin under his fingers. An inhalation of her mildly spicy scent. Sweet lips, slightly cool to his touch at first. The perfect blend of moisture and firmness. Pretty much what he'd fantasized. But he hadn't figured on not being able to stop. No woman had ever birthed wishes in him of becoming a pirate, but his main sail demanded hoisting.

He slanted his head to deepen the kiss. He ran his tongue along the seam of her lips, asking for more, knowing he couldn't settle for less. Her mouth opened on a sigh, he swept into her wet welcome. His bold, uncontrollable tongue explored every nook, every cranny, acting as if it held a D.D.S. degree. As his arms flexed around her, his leg pushed between hers, his hands claiming her backside. She moaned. A wave of possessiveness raged through him, shaking his equilibrium. The flotsam left behind demanded he pull himself together. He lightened the kiss, ending it by gently pulling her bottom lip between his teeth. Feeling he'd hit the eye of the storm, he took a deep breath and leaned back

His fingertips rested on her carotid artery. Her pulse leaped under his touch while his heart pounded along in tune. This was a cardio workout he could get behind in a big way.

He rested his chin on the top of her head, pulling her against his chest, not ready to release her. Their conflagration took place on a public street. He didn't really care, he was too happy to have his fantasy come true, but he needed to think about Abby. She hadn't liked the attention they'd gotten just walking to the theater together. What a dumbass he was sometimes. She'd never want to see him again because he embarrassed her. Damn it.

****

Abby's world tilted at a crazy angle. How had she moved from hoping for a simple goodnight kiss to becoming a boneless wonder? She remembered thinking, *Oh, goodie, he's going to kiss me. Now what should I do?*

Next thing she knew she was two seconds from climbing the man. Of course, he was hard as a rock in ways she hadn't expected. But no excuse. Had it been the tips of his fingers grazing along her throat or his aptitude for nibbling her neck? Or the heat that enfolded and comforted her? Perhaps she'd gone too long without a man. Whatever the reason, if there was only one reason, she'd lost control.

Her hands ran a cross-country race, wanting to

memorize all of his hills and valleys at first touch. And the highways. Not to mention the power pole located in the lower half of his geography. The pole that must be part of an erector set because it kept on growing. She craved this man more than morning coffee.

He pulled her against his chest. She glanced around; the street appeared empty. She took a breath. Maybe no one had seen them.

But she'd noticed. What a kiss. Kiss? More like seismic activity. Time had jumped, just a nanosecond, but it definitely jerked. Abby had felt it happen as their lips met. The air around them shifted too, in an indefinable way. Definitely the world tilted. She gazed at Carlos from under her eyelashes. What did he think? She eased back within the circle of his muscled arms.

Carlos executed a neat turn, tucking her snugly at his side, his arm around her shoulders. He stood with his head thrown back. Sure, she thought, he regretted kissing her. Maybe he thought her way too grabby.

"Abby, I'm sorry, I didn't mean to embarrass you on the street like this. I apologize."

She turned to face him. "No, you didn't do anything wrong." She bit her lower lip. "I don't date much, so I—"

Carlos reversed her position, again pulling her against his chest. "I'm sorry about the location, but, oh, hell, I can't stop myself."

His lips booked hers for a return engagement. Her knees buckled. A small part of her brain still attempted rational thought. Was Blue Peak on a fault line? This surely felt like an earthquake. Her rational mind gave itself to exploring seismic activity of the sensual kind.

Chapter Nineteen

Abby studied the arrangement of multi-colored roses a deliveryman had handed her minutes ago. Bunny stood next to her, head tipped with curiosity. Her hands shook as she placed the vase on the kitchen counter. Pink tea roses nestled next to crimson long-stemmed roses, which sat beside white floribunda and yellow grandiflora roses. The bouquet incorporated other roses as well, including all the colors and types she'd planned for her mural and the floor.

She pulled the card out of the attached envelope then saw a flash of color at the back door.

Sally knocked and walked in casually. "Hey Abby, how was the movie?" She placed the plate of cookies she'd brought with her next to the flowers and fluffed Bunny's ears.

Abby jammed the card into her pocket. "I loved it. What a wonderful film. I know I'll look at life differently, especially because what society calls insanity isn't always crazy. Wow, cookies, thanks."

She hoped the innocent expression she'd attempted worked with her heated face.

"And did Carlos act like a gentleman?"

"Yes. We had a nice time. What else do you want to know?"

"Oh, nothing, just that you've got a beautiful floral arrangement sitting on your counter and I'm wondering if it came from someone I know and gave birth to."

She hoped Sally wouldn't ask to see the card. There was no telling what had been written on it.

"Oh, yes. They just arrived."

Sally's lips quirked. "Sooo, who sent them?"

Abby made a show of looking for the card she'd stashed. "I don't see a card."

"You put it in your pocket."

Shoot. "Carlos. How sweet. You taught him well." She returned the card to hiding.

Sally snorted. "He didn't learn how to womanize from me, I guarantee you."

"So you think the flowers are part of a game?"

Sally drew Abby into a hug. "No, sweetie, not at all. I've never known Carlos to send flowers after the first date. And believe me, I'd have heard. He's decided," she added in an undertone.

Abby sucked in a breath. She wouldn't consider Sally's last comment. Carlos had paid attention to her and her plans. He appreciated her art. She stared at the flowers without really seeing them.

"Not much gets past the electric grapevine in this town. So tell me, is he a good kisser?"

"For crying out loud, Sally. I don't kiss and tell, especially to a man's mother."

Sally raised her eyebrows at that declaration. "I teased, but I think the answer is yes." She mumbled to herself. "Like his father."

"Regardless that these were sent by your son, don't you think this is a bit much after one date?"

"Sweetie, you two have been dancing around each other from the start. Besides, you deserve the best, and in my book, that's Carlos."

Abby's voice betrayed her confusion. "But how do I know he's the best? How do I know he won't walk out? How do I know he's really interested in me?"

Bunny sat on Abby's left foot, leaning her head against Abby's leg.

Sally's smile faded. "You don't know, sweetie, no one can say. But I'll tell you what I know about Carlos. He has high standards. Females have chased him for years but you're the first woman he's been serious about since, well, in a while."

Sally's tone made Abby curious. "Is there something I should know?"

"That's for him to tell you, and soon." She leaned against the counter. "Abby, take what comes. I know you think I'm just an old hippie, but love really is all there is."

Abby spoke softly. "Beauty and thorns. I don't want more heartache."

Sally lightly tapped her fingernails on the counter. "I can't tell you that he won't hurt you, but I hope you'll take a chance on love." She stopped tapping and crossed her arms. "You're too young to hide out alone. Give Carlos, no, give *yourself* an opportunity. That's all."

A few moments passed in silence.

Her friend roused herself, shaking her head slightly. "You're braver than you know."

"Me?" She hid her face by bending to lift Bunny.

Sally grasped her by the forearm, squeezing lightly. "Yes, you. You invested almost everything you have in pursuit of your dreams. Then you shortened your name against your mother's life-long brain washing, and now you're considering putting your heart on the line. Those acts take courage."

The familiar sense of denial raised its head. "It really wasn't any big deal. I just couldn't stay where I was anymore." Bunny licked her on the jaw.

Sally shook her head again, stronger this time. "Sweetie, do you have any idea how many people remain in bad situations because they're afraid to change?"

She placed her lips against Bunny's fur. That hadn't occurred to her. At the time, the move had seemed more like escape than courageous behavior.

"You took steps to make your dreams come true, Abby. That's not escape, that's brave."

Once again Sally read her mind. She'd have to learn to mask her thoughts.

"Don't forget to pull that card out of your pocket before you do your laundry."

She tucked Bunny onto her hip, reaching into her pocket as the door clicked shut behind Sally. Would she never have privacy again?

Her stomach churned as she clasped the card with shaking hands. She reread the words.

"Time stood still."

She grabbed the edge of the counter, knees weak, heart pounding. Damn.

****

"Woo-hoo, Sally. Your friend of a friend came through. I've got the official okay to move in."

A chuckle sounded across the telephone line. "Shame on you. You doubted the power of the Universe? I'm telling you, girlfriend, you are meant to live next door to me."

Abby loosened her grip on the phone. "I guess

you're right. My hurdles disappeared thanks to you. This is the smoothest job I've ever run."

"All I did was make a call or two. You're the one who put the work in every day. Now it's time to celebrate. Tonight. My place. I'll call Carlos."

Carlos? Her stomach churned. Facing the man who'd kissed her senseless? In front of his mother? "Sally, no. I mean, not a good idea with moving tomorrow."

"You need to lighten up, but I understand. We'll let loose after the move. See you tomorrow, bright and early."

Abby leaned against the kitchen counter. Sally had talked with her about the power of females. Of bonding and working together for a greater good. She'd half-scoffed, but with Sally's contacts, this job came together in record time. She knew she had the strength and dedication to make it in a man's world. Rich and all the interfering men could go suck eggs.

****

A small group waited when Abby pulled up to her storage facility the next morning. A quick hour passed resulting in a filled rental van. Sally and Carlos had also packed their cars with boxes, leaving an empty storage unit.

She jumped into the vehicle with a smile. Some might think her lack of furniture sad. Abby preferred to think her limited belongings equated to a blank canvas. Her favorite books, music, art, and special inherited furniture were the basics upon which she'd build her new life.

An active whirlwind had her belongings inside and placed before she knew what had happened. Carlos had taken every opportunity to touch Abby as they exchanged items. He brushed by her, trailing his hand lightly down her arm.

No man had ever played with her in this light-hearted, sweet way before. She decided to let go and have fun. Yes, her life was changing, and what a revolution. She'd played along with him, and took opportunities to trade touches when she thought no one could see them. When she'd gone inside to get bottles of water for everyone, he'd jumped to help. Now he'd caged her within his arms against the counter. The refrigerator door stood open. Forgotten.

"I really enjoyed our time together the other night." That's the best she could do?

"Me too. Let me show you." He leaned toward her, his pupils all black, muscles bunching. His lips hovered above hers.

"Hey, what's taking you so long?" Sally said. "I feel like a roll of tape, sticky, sticky, sticky. Oh, sorry, did I interrupt you? Carry on. I'm leaving." She winked and turned away.

Abby's face burned red hot. She wished she could leave with Sally.

Carlos ran his fingers over her cheeks. "We'll pick this up later, okay?"

She nodded. *If I don't die of embarrassment first.*

Carlos stalled until only he and Abby remained in the house. "I noticed you don't have much in the way of larger pieces. Don't you have living room furniture or a bedroom suite?"

"I left that behind. A new bedroom suite should arrive today."

"You want help setting up the bed?"

"The delivery guys will handle the job."

"Hmm. Well how about a mattress checker? I'm certified."

"I bet you are."

"Let me give you my testimonial."

He grabbed her waist and pulled her closer. Avoiding her lips, he lavished open-mouthed kisses from her ear down to and along her jaw. He continued his route across her jaw with sporadic drops to her throat. He paid attention to her neglected ear. Her lips, still untouched, trembled.

Fresh tobacco smoke. She froze. Gordon hadn't shown for days and chose now to return. Carlos halted mid-kiss to look a question at her.

She peeled herself off him and said, "Ah, I hate to say this but I need to get the truck back, I only rented it for the morning. And I must smell to high heaven, I'd really like to shower."

He gifted her with a blank stare and swallowed. "Tom at the rental place is a friend of mine, and a coffee house regular. I'll ask him to let you go with a warning." He reached for her, pulled her against him, and nibbled on her lips. "And don't you know that sweat turns guys on? Or didn't you notice." He pressed an impressive bulge against her stomach.

The tobacco smell grew stronger in her nostrils. "Um, well, I'm worried about Bunny. I don't want her caught by the landlord, but I also didn't want her stepped on during the move. In fact, I should go pick her up right now." Her voice wavered nervously.

"You won't escape me."

"I don't want to escape."

Carlos leaned back. "I should go. I'm covering the

afternoon shift."

She inhaled, unsure if she felt relieved or disappointed. "We can celebrate a job well done and relax tonight."

"Let's eat at my house. I'd like you to visit. Plus, Bunny can run with Henry in the yard."

A whiff of tobacco odor teased her nostrils again.

"Fine, but I insist on providing dinner. I can take a break from work tonight thanks to everyone's help."

"Sweetheart," Carlos replied, "the break I have in mind isn't restful but I guarantee you'll feel better." He sauntered for the door, obviously recognizing an exit line when he spoke one.

Chapter Twenty

Once she'd heard Carlos drive off, Abby blasted Gordon. "What are you doing? Can't a girl have a social life without you butting in? And for that matter, where have you been? I haven't heard from you for days. Now you show up? Now?"

"I saw what you were up to in here. Nice girls don't—"

"Nice girl? Who said I'm a nice girl? What gave you that impression?" Abby looked for a paper bag to breathe in to. Her breath caught in her chest.

"Now, Abby—"

"Don't you 'now Abby' me. You've got no right to come in here and bust up my love life. No sir, none. You're not my father."

Intense silence fell in the room and in her head.

"Is that who put your back up?"

"No." At least, he wasn't the only one. *Nosy ghost.*

"Girlie, I've been watching you work way too hard. You barely trust yourself. And now you're head over heels for some guy you scarcely know. I'm concerned, that's all. I don't want to see you get hurt. But I get it, you don't want me around. I'm just a ghost. What do I know?"

"I'm not head over heels. Oh, for crying out loud. Did you take Guilt 101 in college?"

"I didn't go to college. I worked my way up the

ladder."

"I was being sarcastic."

"I know."

"If you treated Julia this way, it's no wonder she left home." Cold air swooped around Abby. Damn, what a low-blow comment. "Okay, truce. Let's reach an agreement. You allow me to have a love life and I help you whenever you're ready to tell me why you're hanging around. How's that?"

"Well—"

"Oh, and since you're still deciding, I want your promise that you won't sneak peeks at me when I'm in the shower or changing clothes."

"What kind of ghost do you take me for? Lydia would have my head if I watched you do personal things."

"Really? So you interrupted me with Carlos, why? And does Lydia know?"

"Now, Abby."

"I warned you about 'now Abby.' What do you have to say for yourself?"

"Ahem."

"Gordon."

"Oh, all right. I'm sorry I stuck my nose in to save you when you didn't want to be saved. Does that make you happy?"

Abby heard him muttering words that sounded like, "You puppy."

"Yes, thank you, Gordon."

"You're welcome. But I still say—"

"Hush."

"Oh, all right."

"Look, you can keep me company if you like. I'm

going upstairs to work in the small bedroom."

"You're making that into your studio, right?"

"How did you know that, Gordon? Have you been inserting yourself into my dreamtime again?"

He made a throat clearing sound. "No, um, I hoped you'd use Lydia's sewing room for your studio. That's all. She always said she had good light in there."

Abby swallowed a dry lump. "Um, thanks for telling me Gordon. Now, let's get busy. Maybe we'll find those letters, yet."

She carted shelving, a short stepladder, tools, and bags of hardware into the bedroom. Once she installed the new wire shelving and hanging baskets, she'd indulge in one of her favorite pastimes—organizing her paint supplies.

Bunny settled in the doorway, her head resting on her paws. Gordon's tobacco odor swirled but he didn't comment.

The first overhead shelf came out easily, but the second, higher one stuck. Grabbing a hammer, she tapped the shelf edges and heard an odd rattle.

"What the heck?"

The short stepladder didn't give her the height she needed to see over the shelf. She found a taller ladder and climbed, ducking her head to fit inside the closet. There in the shelf's corner sat a small, dark wooden box.

Her breath caught. No way.

Abby grasped the box and lifted but it didn't move. Stuck. No wonder no one noticed it tucked into the corner.

She worked the shelf loose and pulled it and the attached box from the closet.

Bunny's head rose from her paws.

"Gordon, is this—?

"Yes, that's Lydia's box. I'm sure she left the letters in there."

Abby studied the container. The lid was embossed with a heart and no other decoration besides a small etched-surface lock. Bunny rose, walking to her, tail held straight out and high, nose sniffing rapidly in the box's direction. The lid was locked and she didn't see a key.

"Gordon, I'm not sure I can free the box without ruining it. Do you know if the key is handy? Maybe we should just open the box so you can have the letters. Or if you don't know where the key is, someone with the right knack could easily pick the lock."

"Abby, leave it for now." His voice held a hoarse undertone. "I need to think about this."

"Think? You've been bugging me for weeks, waiting to find this box. Now you're changing your mind?"

"No, I'm not backing out. It's just that, well, I thought Lydia would appear with the box. She's not here and like I said, I'm not going anywhere without her."

Abby inhaled through her nose. If anyone understood fear of the unknown, it was herself. What a pair the two of them made.

"I understand. Um, Gordon, do you mind if I take the board and box to the hardware store? Maybe someone there could help me with this problem. I'm more accustomed to tearing down and rebuilding than the fine work this requires."

"Oh, all right. Just don't mess up."

She knew the small wooden box's origins had a history but didn't press Gordon.

"Be back in a while." Tobacco odor and no flippant comment in response. He had to be shaken to his misty core.

Later, she returned and placed the still locked box, now separated from the shelf, on her new stove top before heading off to shower and change for her date.

Gordon had the box and would dictate the next step. Her part in this whodunit was complete.

The next mystery facing her was whether she should sleep with Carlos, if they progressed to that point. And the follow-up mystery, would he'd think her a slut for jumping him first.

Chapter Twenty-One

Carlos lived in a stone-faced house with a small but neat yard. He sat on his porch with Henry on the floor beside him. Henry's ears pricked forward when he spotted Bunny then he ran to greet her. Setting his long-necked bottle of beer down, Carlos rose and met Abby in the yard.

She scanned his length. He'd slicked back his hair, his clothes were neatly pressed. Tonight he wore a Rockabilly-style shirt in soft gray with dark gray embroidered roses above the double pocket flaps. The shirt's color enhanced his eyes while showing off his wide shoulders and flat stomach. When Carlos took the basket from her, she checked her chin for drool.

His thumb rubbed against the back of her hand. "What's all this? There's enough here for a couple of days."

"Sally flagged me down. I'm not sure what she packed, but it's a 'first night' gift. I thought I'd share with you."

"Are you hungry?" His deep voice sucked at her restraint, tore at her caution.

"I'd be more hungry inside, I think. Your neighbors are curious, aren't they?" A curtain snapped back into place at the window of his neighbor's house.

He rubbed her cheek. "You've got a lot to learn about life in a small town." He called the dogs. They trotted inside and settled in the kitchen.

She stopped in the kitchen doorway, watching his hand dip into the basket.

"Do we start with appetizers or dessert?" Carlos eyed the whipped cream and fresh strawberries now placed on the counter. "I'm partial to dessert."

A dry lump invaded her throat. "I think, maybe, uh…yes, dessert is good."

Plucking a berry between thumb and forefinger, he sauntered to her then poised the fruit above her lips. "Like a taste?"

Him or the fruit?

Lightly puckered red flesh brushed her lips and the sweet aroma nudged her salivary glands. He rubbed the strawberry against the seam of her lips, teasing them open. As she bit in, flavor exploded and juice ran down her chin. Before she could lick it up, he was there, his tongue swiping her chin, followed by an open- mouthed kiss to her neck.

"Mmm, now that was a tasty treat."

The fleeting touch of a cotton napkin left dry skin behind. *No, no, no—keep the kisses coming—forget the damn napkin.*

Strawberry-scented fingers brushed her cheek as darkened eyes caught her gaze.

"But on second thought, I really like appetizers." His glance flicked to her lips. "I could make a meal ofn'em."

Saliva instantly filled Abby's mouth. That low, dark voice of his made a tasty appetizer all its own. Then add in the large male thumbs rubbing lazy circles on her hips for spice. Their lips met. Yes, and a taste of sugar.

He plastered himself against her. For an instant she lost her boundaries, unable to differentiate her body from his. The tip of his tongue tasted the corner of her lips then retreated.

"A good start is important to a meal."

She swallowed, waiting for his next comment.

His lips barely touched the soft skin behind her ear. "Maybe we should take our time."

Her back arched as he licked the outside curve of her ear, blew on it and nibbled along her neck and jaw to her other ear.

"Balanced meals are important, too."

As he repeated the licking, blowing and nibbling, she had to agree with whatever it was that he'd said. Her knees buckled. She couldn't catch a deep breath.

"What-guh-guh-guh?" Abby sputtered. "You've got me stuttering like Porky Pig."

Carlos raised his head, mouth stretched in a wicked grin. "Trust me. You look nothing at all like Porky Pig."

Shivers followed his fingertips down her spine. Contracted muscles followed them back up. His lips brushed over her temples, briefly lighting against her closed eyelids.

Her befuddled senses cleared, reminding her that they'd planned a dinner for two. She pressed her lips against his freshly shaven cheeks and strong jaw. Her tongue moved up the side of his neck to his ear, darting along the whorl, the scent of his soap filling her nostrils.

His mouth to her ear he whispered, "So have you decided?" And blew.

She gasped. "De-decided?"

"Appetizer or dessert?"

"You know …I don't … you leave me speechless."

"Do you mind?" he asked, dribbling kisses over her jaw in the same rat-a-tat-tat rhythm as her heart.

"Should I stop?" He paused, nuzzling the soft well between her collarbones, sending her senses into orbit. "Tell me now."

His movement forced her eyes open. "Don't stop." His lips returned to hers. *Ever.*

A flush of cool air contracted her nipples as he peeled himself away.

He removed his glasses, placing them on the counter. Resting his forehead on hers he rubbed his hand along her arm. "You've been working hard all day. Don't you want to get off your feet? Let's move into the living room."

She ducked, grabbed the wine glasses, and bottle. "Bring the basket."

"I love it when you're demanding."

Abby grinned and swayed her hips as she sauntered toward the hallway. She took three steps before she was swung into his arms and pulled against his chest.

"A three-fer. You, the wine and the glasses in one sweep. I'm pretty damn good."

"Big talker. You haven't proved anything, yet." Her face heated. *Geez, she'd turned into a slut.* "Sorry. I don't know what's gotten into me."

"Nothing, yet. Me, soon, I hope." His lips came down on hers, his tongue pushing against the seam of her lips. "Tell me if I move too fast for you."

Arm muscles bunched under her thighs. The aroma of roses filled her nostrils. She sensed they moved then she sank into soft down-filled cushions. Her breath whooshed out. His length pressed against her.

"It's all I can do to hold myself back from eating you up."

She watched him, unsure if he teased her again.

"You look doubtful." He rubbed his thumb across her lips. "I take that as a personal insult." He replaced his thumb with his lips. "Let me show you how good we'll be."

Abby's breath hitched.

"I'll take it slow." He ran his fingers up and across her collarbone, then wove back down over her breasts, lightly grazing her nipples, never alighting. Then his other hand joined the first and together they covered each of her breasts, rubbing lightly.

His eyes darkened. "Slow enough for you?"

She shook her head. "Too slow. I want to see you."

Carlos groaned. "You're not making this easy." He gently removed her shirt then pulled open the snaps of his in one move. His dark gaze met hers as he unsnapped his sleeves and shrugged out of his shirt.

He rubbed his chest against hers. His soft hair abraded her nipples hardening the tips. "Told ya. We're made for each other."

Her inner slut answered. "Talk, talk talk."

He nudged his hard member against her hip. "You make me hot." His gaze seared her. "I wanted slow with you the first time. Ain't happening if you keep mouthing off."

"I've always wanted to be a bad girl."

"Then let me help you make your wish come true."

He covered her torso with kisses. She wiggled under him as he planted his mouth everywhere but over the nipples pleading for his attention. Abby pulled his mouth over her breast. He sucked her nipple, swirling his tongue around her peak.

If he hadn't been pressed over her, she'd have come off the couch with the sensation. A heated spiral moved into her core. She moved her hands over his buttocks and grabbed.

He moaned. "I'm at your command." He kissed the soft skin under her chin. "Tell me your desires." He licked a path back to her nipple. "Anything, as long as it's me in you sooner than later." He pulled one breast into his mouth while covering the other with his palm.

She shifted her hips, plastering herself against him. One hand caressed his buttocks through his slacks while the other traced his spine.

Her scalp tingled as his fingers smoothed her hair. She ran her finger around his ear down his jaw, dancing over his cheeks, feeling his heat overtake her. Essence of a spicy soap and hot musk wafted to her nostrils.

She wanted to jump out of her skin to avoid the heat. Then she gave in and let their steamy, slick intensity rule. "I can't wait. I need you. All of you."

His hand moved between them. Abby heard and felt her zipper lowering, then he lifted his body away and she balanced while he pushed her jeans off.

Her hands shook with need as she helped him move his slacks over his butt. She stilled. "Commando?"

His shaft pressed against her stomach. "I'm a positive thinker."

She pushed against his chest. "Well, Mr. Thinker. Don't forget the condom, because I don't want to test positive."

"Got it." He pulled a foil packet from his slacks pocket. "Want to help?"

Abby took the packet, ripping it open using her teeth and one hand. "I read an article about women using their mouths to put on a man's condom." She felt his penis jerk under her hand.

"We may not need that condom if you don't shut up and put it on me. Now."

"Maybe I should try that move some other time." She rolled the latex down his length.

"I can't wait to dive in to your sweet, wet heat. Okay with you?"

"Promises, promises." She hadn't finished speaking when he pushed into her in one long glide. Carlos filled her and more.

Raspy breaths filled her hearing while a musky scent overwhelmed her nostrils.

Her eyelids fluttered closed as his fingers gripped her outer thighs, keeping her in place as he pumped into her wetness. Pinioned, she squeezed her inner muscles around his penis. His pace increased, and she pushed her feet against the cushion, lifting her hips in unison against his, taking him deeper.

Sweaty bodies slapped skin to skin, the scent of arousal grew.

"Open your eyes and look at me, Abby. We're knocking on heaven's door. Watch."

Carlos rubbed her clit as his mouth covered hers, his tongue demanding, his finger pushing, rubbing. His back arched, and he moved to fill her more completely.

"Oh, God! Oh! Yes!"

Her convulsive shudders triggered Carlos into climaxing a second later. They gazed at each other with enlarged pupils, sucking warm, humid air redolent with their mixed come.

Carlos bent his head, lightly nipping her jaw. "Wow, lady."

"Mmmmm."

He nuzzled her neck then slid out. "'Scuse me, sweet one. Gotta make a quick bathroom run. Be ready to cuddle when I return."

His butt didn't shake, wiggle or quiver as he strolled away, pausing at the doorway to wink over his shoulder at her. As he disappeared around the corner she stretched.

The cool air brought a sense of reality. What the hell had she just done? Besides having the best sex of her life?

Feet rustled across the carpet then the cushions dipped as he sat down next to her. His arm encircled her tense shoulders. She grabbed an afghan off the couch, wanting to shield herself for her bathroom walk.

"My turn."

"Hurry back."

In the bathroom with the door closed behind her, she clutched at her chest, trying to slow her Mach Two heartbeat. She ran the hot water while searching her reflection. Her sexually satisfied self.

Abby performed her ablutions then slumped on the closed toilet, her forearms resting on her thighs. She tried to work out her next steps. First, cover her tracks. Pretend this was nothing special or he'd think her needy, falling for him after one bout of sex. She stood, nodded to her mirrored self and walked into the living room.

"I can't believe that happened." Oops. Not what she'd planned on saying.

"You're disappointed?"

"No, no, not at all. I mean, I guess I must have buried my sex drive, but it sure came back in spades with you, tonight."

Too much information. She needed to get some help with small talk. Or maybe she meant after sex talk.

"Abby, I love your sexiness and I'm really glad it came back in spades tonight, with me." He leered at her and said, "I'll be your gardener anytime, baby."

"I can dig that," she blew out a breath. Maybe she could do this after all. Keep joking, don't show him how much he mattered already and everything would be okay.

"You want to play in the dirt, maybe get to the root of your concerns?"

She encircled his penis with two fingers. "I'll play with your spade anytime." His penis stood up for her.

"That was a great appetizer. Ready for dinner?" His hand reached toward the condoms on the floor.

"I think it's my turn as chef." She nudged the afghan off and moved atop Carlos. The world disappeared.

Chapter Twenty-Two

Abby woke feeling warm and relaxed. Rolling onto her side, she brushed against a lean male body. She opened her eyes. Oh, dear God, she'd had sex with Carlos. More than once.

Had she made a gigantic mistake? Their lovemaking had cemented her feelings about him. She had no more doubts about her emotional investment with the man lying next to her. She did, however, wonder if he returned her feelings. Damn. She'd just set herself up for one big failure. And she'd seen the crash coming for way too long.

He appeared asleep. Good, she couldn't face him right now. She'd get dressed and leave. She inched to her side of the bed but Carlos clamping his arm over her torso stopped her move.

He nuzzled her ear. "Good morning, Abby," he whispered.

Her nipples hardened. Her hips rose slightly. Her toes curled. This man didn't make her body wonder if she'd made a mistake. Her skin had gone on high alert. She may have doubts, but her body knew exactly what it wanted. More sex.

"Who are you?" she mock demanded. "My body was abducted by aliens in the night. I've never acted like this before."

"How's that?" He rubbed her nipples, circling them

with his fingers.

"Wanton. I feel like a wanton woman." That was more true than she'd verbally admit. She had discovered an immediate sexual honesty with Carlos that she'd never had with Rich. Most likely because the emotional tie with Carlos was already stronger than she'd had with her ex, even after their ten years of marriage.

She caressed his chest and arms, moving her hands lightly over him, thrilled when his muscles tightened in response. "And what are you wantin'? I bet I can fill your need." He moved his hand from her breasts to her stomach.

"Hmmm. I might be wantin' a fill-up. Can you help?" She stroked his growing penis.

"I aim to please." He licked his lips, cleared his throat. "Want me to check under the hood for you? Your oil might be a little low."

He smoothed his fingers across her thighs and inner lips. She was already wet.

"Ah, I think my oil is topped off."

"How about your windows, ma'am? I've got a brand new squeegee I'd like to try out." He lightly thumbed her sensitive nub.

"Just the fill will do for now."

And it did.

They cuddled in the middle of the bed when she saw his clock. "Six thirty! I never stay in bed this long. I've got work to do today. And what about the coffee house? Don't you have to open your business? Aren't you tired?"

"Hey, I'm a stamina machine." He yawned. "I can work without sleep. Although it helps that I own multiple coffee machines. And that I can call in an employee to cover for me, which I did after we walked the dogs last night."

"If you won't be at Collective Unconscious, you can help me at the house." She froze. "That is, if you don't have something else planned." She'd said more than she meant to, again. Nothing drove off a man faster than a needy female.

"I'd love to help."

The dogs traipsed into the room angling for food. Their demands were met and as the four left for Abby's, she ignored the shifted window curtains in houses up and down the block.

****

Abby's tongue flicked out to lick her lower lip. "What?"

He grinned inwardly as he donned the most innocent expression in his repertoire. "What, what?"

She huffed. "Stop being such a man and answer my question. Why are you watching me? You haven't heard a word I've said."

"You're easy on the eyes."

Her face remained pinched. Carlos hated that scared look. Ah, but if she hadn't had issues, she wouldn't be here with him. He'd wipe that look away, for good.

"Let's sit outside. The sun may even break through the clouds today."

They settled on the porch. He folded her hands in his. "Abby, do you know why I enjoy your company?"

She shook her head.

"Besides the fact that you're intelligent and beautiful, you don't try to change people. I've watched you with others. You accept others as they are, without judgment. I can't begin to tell you how many women have tried to change me to fit their rules for life."

"You?" She shifted. "Why would anyone want to change perfection?"

"Most women I've met think puns are juvenile."

"Well then they obviously have no appreciation for Shakespeare."

"You like Shakespeare?" He'd never met a woman better suited to him. Careful, he reminded himself. Go slow. And find a way to tell her he'd been helping behind the scenes.

She nodded. "So did my ex, Rich." Her face fell.

"Do you want to share any of what happened?" He held his breath as she hesitated.

Giving a sigh as if she'd reached a tough decision she said, "Yes, well, maybe it's time, and I think you can help me understand the man's view. Because I certainly don't get it."

"I don't know if I'll give you a man's view, but I'll tell you what I think." He slid his arm around her shoulders.

"Rich moved on emotionally much faster than I did. He began dating a woman days after we'd separated. Before we'd legally filed for divorce." She flipped her palm up like a traffic cop. "I know, I know, some men can't stand to be alone. But I wondered if they were together before we split. It was so quick, you know? Plus, she got pregnant right away."

She remained quiet and he didn't push her. "Ten years together and I was replaced within two weeks. How is that possible? How can men do that?"

No whine—she asked it straight out. He pulled her

close and kissed her briefly. "I don't know how he could do that to you. People do nasty things to each other. It's not your fault it happened."

"I guess. Now it's your turn."

He hesitated. She'd turned the discussion to him a little too fast. He decided not to push her. "Are you sure you want to hear this?"

She nodded.

"I was engaged for about five years to a colleague at the college. We were both in the Psych Department and I thought we had similar interests. Certainly we had the same friends and understood each other's work. We had plenty to talk about at the end of the day."

Carlos planted a kiss on her neck. "I wanted marriage, a family, white picket fence, the works. Sierra, well, I thought she wanted the same even though we never talked about it in detail. We fit on so many levels it was difficult for me to understand that she wasn't the person I pictured in my head. You know, if you're talking you must be communicating, right?"

Abby worried her lower lip. He wondered what bothered her. Was it something he said? She nudged him.

"Obviously, I lived in another world. Sierra never wanted to set a wedding date or look at houses together. When I pushed for resolution, she pushed back. Said she needed 'space to think.' She went out of town for the summer break and came back married to a mutual colleague. They don't have a house or kids. That's when I looked at my priorities, quit teaching and bought the coffee house."

"You loved her so much you couldn't stand to see her married to your friend, right? Don't you miss teaching just as intensely? I've seen you mentoring students. You look at ease with them. Like explaining concepts is an integral part of you."

He shrugged. "That's behind me." Was it? Wasn't he lying to her and himself? He hadn't yet made up his mind about what direction to take.

"Would you return to the college if they offered?"

His muscles tightened. What did she know? Had someone told her about Sierra coming back?

"Well, I'd think about the opportunity." *Tell her. Talk it out with her. She understands. What would she think about Sierra's reappearance?*

Clearing his throat, he submerged his instinctual need to confide all the details. "Actually, I recently heard about an opening. I may have a chance to return."

"That's great! You could pick up a class or two and still run the coffee house, right?"

"Maybe I could do both." He'd been thinking all of one or the other. Handling both jobs would be a cinch if Sierra and Jillian would leave him be. Working two jobs and dating? How could he give his all in three different directions? He could, actually, if Abby were involved.

"Unless seeing your ex-fiancée would be too painful?"

He shook his head. "Sierra? Not painful anymore. Lately I've been thinking about taking a new direction. I'd like to spend the rest of my life with a special woman. Maybe have babies together."

He struggled to keep his heart from showing in his eyes.

Her lips quirked, rising slightly at the corners. "Your mother will be over the moon."

Did she really not understand what he meant? He pushed his disappointment aside. "Promise me you won't say anything to her."

She examined her nails. "My silence comes at a high cost."

"I'll make a down payment with dinner. I've got meat and vegetables for the grill. How'd you like kebobs to eat? We can discuss your blackmail demands after dinner."

"But there's so much left to do here. You promised you'd help, and today's chore list isn't complete."

"Abby, you allow that damn list to rule your life." He spat out "list." "Can't you play with me a little?" He grabbed her, nuzzled her neck.

She moved away. "I've got to get this place finished. Sure, Sally helped me with City Hall, and the contractors fell into place faster than I thought. But I'm sick of unsettled homes and having people think I'm only good for organizing paperwork."

His stomach dropped. "Is that what Rich did?"

She nodded. "He made it clear that I wasn't the heavy hitter in our partnership. I need to see this project through, to prove I can handle the work." She took his hand. "It means a lot to me, and I'm glad you understand."

Shit. He understood, all right. He'd screwed up trying to help. He needed to tell her how he'd interfered immediately. "Abby, I—"

"So let's finish the next three items then break for supper."

"Yes, okay." He'd tell her after dinner. His news would go down better with wine. Lots of wine and plenty of hot sex. Maybe she'd be in a forgiving frame

of mind. He hoped she'd let him live.
****

Bunny led the way into her house, darting in front of Henry the next morning. Abby walked into the kitchen then stopped, puzzled. She'd left the wooden box on the stovetop but now it lay positioned in the middle of her sketchbook, over the study of roses she'd done for the floor. Gordon at work, again.

"Carlos?"

"Right here. What's up?"

"I've got a story to tell you."

"Ah, you wait until I'm your sex slave before you reveal you're wanted in three states for murder and armed robbery." He hung his head. "I never could pick women."

Sex slave? Must be his joke. Plus, she'd better not think about sex right now.

"No, it's not that." She rubbed her arms. "You may not like my story. You told me you don't believe in ghosts, right?"

"True. I did."

His gaze caught hers but she couldn't read his expression.

"But I also said ghosts are possible. Try me. I'll listen to your tale."

Her stomach clenched. "My house has a ghost. It's Gordon Wilkinson."

His face remained expressionless. "Go on."

Abby swallowed hard. He wasn't making this easy. She clasped her hands in front of her to keep them still. "Yes, well I can't see him, I can only smell his tobacco smoke and hear him, sometimes as if someone spoke to me, other times as strong thoughts in a man's voice."

She smiled faintly. "You'd probably consider them hallucinations."

Their silence grew. She uttered a small distressed sound. He touched her arm.

"You know, I've been thinking about ghosts and the paranormal." He rubbed the back of his neck. "I think I told you that living with my mom made me nuts. She operates from her heart most of the time."

"You act from your heart more than you think."

He held up his hand, palm out. "Maybe, but I believe science is king. Well, besides Elvis, who's the real King."

She rubbed her arm. "I figured you'd think I'm nuts. At least let me finish the renovation before you report me."

Carlos shook his head. "You're not any crazier than I am. And definitely less nutty than my mom." He shifted. "Psychology doesn't have the ultimate answers for life's mysteries. There's much we don't know, and to slap a label on what we don't understand doesn't help people or science."

He looked directly into her eyes. "You are one of the most down-to-earth people I know. You work way too hard, but I'd be happy to advise you on how to change." His lips curved into a brief smile.

"But you still don't believe in ghosts."

"Nope. Sorry. But don't let me change your beliefs and don't hide your thoughts." He blew out a breath. "Mom sure doesn't."

"So you can't smell tobacco smoke?"

"Nuh, uh."

"You don't hear a man's voice calling you a puppy?"

"Can't say as I do."

She sighed. "Well then, it's been fun."

He grasped her upper arms. "Oh, no. You won't get away from me and I won't let you back off from us."

"I'm not backing off."

"Really?"

She had to be honest with this man. "Okay, maybe I am scared."

"And you think I'm not?" He rubbed her arms. "I'm big enough to let you have your beliefs. I don't believe in ghosts but you can. No big deal." He kissed her. "Didn't I tell you about my secret bent for quantum mechanics? We live in a multi-verse where all things are possible."

"Sally tried to explain something similar to me. I didn't understand."

"So let's teach each other. Don't let old beliefs get in the way."

Abby wasn't sure she could compromise about ghosts. She knew Gordon was as real as anything else in the room, even if she couldn't see him. Then there was Carlos's habit of taking over. He seemed better, but once a boss, always a control freak.

She kissed him knowing they had some battles ahead. This time, though, she'd stick to her guns. Maybe their new relationship would work and maybe it wouldn't. There was no way to know unless she gave it a shot.

****

Carlos wondered how he'd ended up with a woman who shared his mother's beliefs. He knew he'd never live this down.

More scientific proof of ghosts was published

every year. Maybe they did exist. He could keep an open mind. The topic wouldn't keep him from enjoying Abby, however long their attraction lasted. If the last few days were an indication, they could be together a long time.

He pulled her tight. "So, what can I do to help around here?"

"You're doing just fine right now."

Now that they'd reached an agreement on the paranormal, he should reveal his interference with her project. He should have told her last night, but she'd fallen asleep after dinner. And this morning she'd been focused on getting back to work. She'd made more friends in town, and his secret wouldn't remain confidential for long. Not in Blue Peak.

Maybe he'd better get one more kiss. Just in case Abby blew a gasket when he told her what he'd done on her behalf.

His lips covered hers then he heard rattling. He pulled back. "Stop goofing around. I'm performing serious work here."

Abby's lips curved. "My arms are around you. Gordon is playing."

"Right." He pressed his lips to hers.

She withdrew. "I'm not kidding."

He chuckled. "Okay." His mouth moved to her ear. He saw the wooden box move on the counter like an unseen hand lifted then set it down.

"Holy shit." He jumped and stepped back. "What the hell?"

"Gordon says watch the blasphemy. He's neither sacred nor feces." She tilted her head just as his mom did when she received her "messages." "And he's not sure about hell. He hasn't seen anything like it since he died." Abby raised one eyebrow. "But ghosts don't exist, right?"

Carlos watched as a smoke-like substance swirled over and around the wooden box. He waited but the mist never coalesced. There were no ghostly facial features or limbs. Then, like a finger snap, he saw a man's outline, wavering around the edges.

"Holy, um, wow."

He shook his head, but the image remained. Could be he suffered from a group hallucination, but there were only two humans in the room. He hadn't eaten anything unusual, so no gastric disturbance. He placed the back of his hand on his forehead. No fever.

Shit. Must be a reflection from the window. Yeah, sun refractions. He glanced outside. Rain. He swallowed a lump the size of Charlotte. The mirage glowed brighter. No way.

Abby placed her hand on his chest. "Are you all right? You look pale."

"Yes, um, yeah I'm fine." *For a crazy man.*

"Gordon says we should open the box."

No way he'd get close to that box, surrounded by light.

"He says there are letters inside that should go to Julia."

"Are you sure?" she said to the wavering image. "He says if the box is locked she won't bother opening it or reading the letters."

He needed to get a grip. What he wanted was to leave by the closest door.

Abby snorted and grabbed the box. He watched the specter move away when she approached then the apparition appeared to lean against the sink.

"I couldn't find a key," she said.

He studied the lock. "I think I can pick this."

"Gordon says he wants me to read the letters before I send them on. Shoot. Are you sure, Gordon?"

Carlos ignored the by-play between Abby and the squiggly white smoke in the room. He requested a thin wire and got to work. He threw the wire onto the counter. "Sorry, but I can't get this. I know a locksmith. He could pop this lock in a heartbeat."

His hands shook. Plus he'd have an excuse to leave and regain control. This scene was not for him. Ghosts. Letters. Prodigal daughters. Gorgeous girlfriends who'd adopted his mom's beliefs. Too many changes too fast.

She nodded. "Sure. I understand. Go ahead and ask your friend to open the lock. Just please don't open the box or check the interior."

"I promise." He shuffled his feet. "I'd better go. Henry needs a run."

"Right. Okay."

"See you later?"

"Only if you want to date a crazy woman." She picked up Bunny and walked out. The ghostly presence dissipated.

He stood still with his hands at his sides. "Damn it." After giving the box an evil glare, he picked it up and left.

****

Ghosts. Damn it. Why did it have to be a ghost?

Carlos sifted through the research pages on his desk. He'd pulled information about ghosts off the Internet. Had he gotten books from his mom, she'd be over here pointing out salient paragraphs for him.

He'd read professional treatises until his eyes burned. Then he'd moved to reports from people who hadn't a scientific bone in their body. All he knew for sure is that the idea of ghosts had been around since the early Egyptians. Unbelievers had likely covered sheets of papyrus with their own ideas in rebuttal.

Hallucinations, air pressure changes, peripheral vision misinterpretations, geomagnetic fields, solar activity, and infrasound were the most prominent explanations for apparition sightings. One research article even cited carbon monoxide poisoning.

Two things he knew for certain. The phantom had appeared during the day not at night, and at a time he wasn't tired or stressed. He could call some guys from the college's science department to get geomagnetic readings, but he didn't want to go there.

Nope, the plain truth—if he wanted to admit it—ghosts existed.

Damn it.

Chapter Twenty-Three

After Carlos left, Abby settled on her lone living room chair, Bunny in her lap. "Gordon? Why do you want me to read Lydia's letters?"

"Because I see you making my mistakes. Just listen, will you?"

"You got it."

"When I was young, money, earning it, obsessed me. I told myself my Lydia deserved money, as much as I could make. You see, we hadn't had any children after seven years, but we never stopped hoping."

Abby thought maybe she understood. But then she remembered Gordon had a daughter. She wondered where his story headed.

"I couldn't handle feeling guilty when I'd see her watch families in the park with that sad look on her face. Work became my escape, and I spent a lot of time there. Too much time there." His voice shook.

"One summer I took a job that kept me out of town for several months. I'd earn a huge bonus. Lydia didn't want me to go and we fought bitterly. It was our first real fight that wasn't settled by the time we went to bed that night. We didn't talk for days, and we still hadn't totally healed the rift before I had to leave. I called daily. Long distance was expensive back then, so I thought Lydia would see how much I cared. She always teased me about my penny pincher habits."

Abby winced. She knew penny pinchers.

"My calls weren't enough because she had an affair. I heard happiness in her voice, and in my conceit, thought I'd been forgiven. I found out I was wrong when I got back and Lydia told me about a fellow she'd met." Her eyes brimmed with tears.

"Reconciling wasn't easy, I'll tell you. Neither of us was proud of the affair, but we learned to live with it. I figured I should shoulder as much blame as Lydia because I'd ignored her. She never told me his name and I never asked. I trusted her that much, you see.

"Later on, we had Julia, named her after my mother, and I loved her, but never as much as Lydia. Only my obsession with money interfered with my love for Lydia. I learned my lesson, I never left town for a long job again. I tried to give Lydia all she needed, but I guess I never could give Julia enough."

Strange, she thought, how Julia's life sounded similar to her own in ways. Her father had rarely been around. She pushed those thoughts out of her mind and concentrated on Gordon.

"Julia withdrew in her teen years, spent almost all her time at school or in her room. Told me I wasn't a father to her. Well, it broke my heart to hear. Old habits die hard, and I avoided the situation by not confronting Julia. It seemed easiest."

"You didn't know how to reach out."

"No, I was just a dang fool," answered Gordon. "Julia left because of my stubbornness. Lydia died of cancer and now I'm lost or could be I was always lost. No matter." She heard the shrug in his answer.

"What I need is for the letters Lydia wrote to get sent to Julia. Any chance that'll happen? Maybe then I can find Lydia and get on with whatever it is I have to do next."

Now she understood why Gordon hung around the house. But the puzzle missed a few pieces. "Carlos took the box with him to the coffee house to ask a locksmith he knows for help."

"Thank you, Abby. You're a good person, do you know that? And that young man of yours is, too. I didn't think so at first. Be good to each other. That's the important thing I learned too late. Talk and stay in touch. Don't let everyday life pull you in opposite directions."

"He may not come back."

"I'm a good judge of character and I know he'll return. Tell him. Don't make my mistakes. Be honest with that man and he'll stay with you through thick and thin."

Once again, Gordon disappeared. She wiped her eyes with her T-shirt and looked for a box of tissues. Gordon's story had hit a little too close to home for her, and in far too many ways. She knew she'd have to take a deeper look at memories but she didn't want to investigate those old wounds. She stumbled outside sinking to the porch and crying out years of hurt and mistrust. Bunny huddled at her side.

Abby pulled herself together as a delivery truck moved down the street toward her house. Her living room suite had arrived. Then her phone rang. The kitchen cabinets were ready for installation.

She collected her tall pile of used tissues and looked for a trash bag. Time to check her project list and get back to work.

****

"Hey, Abby."

"Carlos?"

"My buddy unlocked the box this morning. Plus, we need to talk. I've got something important to tell you that can't wait. If you get a chance, come on by. Sorry, but the place is jammed. Bye."

She couldn't leave, either, finally walking in to the Collective Unconscious Café in the late afternoon.

Jillian's hard stare from across the coffee house made Abby's skin crawl. She rotated her shoulders to shake off her tension.

Being hated even though they'd never met left her feeling creeped out. She understood Jillian's disappointment—they'd both wanted Carlos and Abby had won out. At least for now. But still. Maybe Jillian had never not gotten what she wanted before now.

"Hi, Carlos. I'm excited about the box being unlocked."

"I'll bet you are. Hang on a minute. I have to fill this order, then we'll go to my office."

Carlos had moved away before the heat of Jillian's stare intensified. She rotated on her stool and saw the woman walking toward her with an unpleasant smile in place. Abby avoided her glare. She didn't want to mess with Jillian's bad loser persona. Not today. Not ever.

She felt a sharp talon scrape across her arm. Looking down, she saw a light trail of red where the acrylic fingernail had traced its path. Her gaze moved from her arm to Jillian's face. She hadn't realized a pretty woman could look so ugly.

"You're that helpless little waif aren't you? The one who lives next to Sally?"

When Abby didn't reply she deepened her nasty

smile. "Your name is Allison, right?"

Reflexes caused her head to move back and forth in a "no" answer even as Jillian continued to speak through her gruesome smile.

"Well, Allison, you may be interested in something I heard just the other day."

The malice personified before her mesmerized like a snake rising from a basket. No flute music required. She knew as a foregone conclusion that she'd be forced to hear what the other woman had to say. Was it too late to stick her fingers in her ears and chant, "I can't hear you?"

"So, Allison."

Abby wanted to screech. The woman's affected drawl bothered her more than the deliberate misnaming.

A low masculine voice said, "Jillian" with a warning tone.

She relaxed as Carlos walked up.

"I'm glad you're here, Carlos. You're sure to like the story I'm telling Little Miss Helpless Waif."

Jillian's fingernail tapped her arm once, twice, three times. She forced herself to sit quietly when every touch of the blood red plastic made her want to run for the bathroom and vomit.

His low voice sharpened and repeated, "Jillian, enough."

Her pulse kicked up. Something was wrong.

She moved to leave but Jillian's long fingers wrapped around her wrist, trapping her hand on the counter.

"You," Jillian said her mouth barely moving, "sit still. You're going to hear what I have to tell you."

She perched on the stool, her joy in the day

destroyed. Chill bumps erupted where the woman's hand covered hers.

Carlos's low voice said quietly, "Jillian, you don't want to do this. Leave it be."

Jillian's voice grated out, "But I can't, darling. Don't you think your clueless friend needs to know the whole truth about her little project?"

The truth? Her gaze flew to Carlos. He glared at Jillian, his posture slumped.

She may not like the delivery but she needed to hear the message.

Carlos gazed into her eyes. "Abby, I meant to tell you today. In fact that's why I asked you to come down. I couldn't find a good time before."

"Tell me—"

Jillian broke in. "Oh, that old excuse. I've heard that before and no doubt your little friend has, too."

She abruptly pulled her hand out from under Jillian's. Looking Carlos directly in the eyes she said, "Ignore her. I am. You can tell me now."

Carlos threw his towel on the back counter and held out his hand. "Will you come into my office?"

Jillian laughed, an oily, hateful sound. "Why not tell her right here? Everyone in town already knows the story. And make sure you tell her about Sierra." The woman laughed again.

Abby decided the sound wasn't any prettier the second time around.

She stood and walked to the end of the counter, shaking Carlos's hand off her shoulder. Leading the way into the office, she sat on a straight backed wooden chair in front of his desk. Henry lifted his head but didn't move.

"Tell me." She mentally shrank, for the tone of her voice sounded like her mother's when her parents had fought.

She cleared her throat and, speaking around a rapidly forming lump, said more softly, "What's so bad that you couldn't tell me earlier? Maybe you should start with Sierra."

Carlos sat behind his desk, then stood and paced. He walked to the corner, grabbed a chair to match the one Abby inhabited, placed it next to hers, and sank down. He reached for her hand.

"Sierra isn't in the picture, not now."

Her eyebrows rose in a prompt.

His thumb caressed the back of her hand. "It's just that she, um, split with her husband when he accepted another post in Arizona. That's the teaching opening at the college. His."

Didn't take a rocket scientist masquerading as a mural artist to see the picture. "It's a package deal, huh? That's what you meant when you said you were considering a new life's direction, right? Get back with that special ex-fiancée of yours and have gorgeous babies."

"No, I wasn't referring to Sierra." He rubbed the back of his neck with his free hand. "You won't believe the truth, that's for damn sure."

She pulled her hand from his. "What's the rest of the tale? The story that everyone else in town already knows?"

His Adam's apple moved. "Abby, I admire you. I think you are incredibly talented and organized."

"And?"

Carlos swallowed. "I want you to know that I took

199

the actions I did to help you, not because I thought you weren't able to do it yourself."

She pulled her hand back, her jaw tight. "What did you do?"

His expression became hunted, his voice dropped in volume. She leaned forward in time to hear him say, "I arranged for you to get help out at the house."

Her voice sounded quiet but dangerous. "You *what*?"

"I called in some favors."

He reached for her, enveloping her cold hands with his own. She sat, too stunned to move.

"Some favors. Like contractors that had been delaying me suddenly showed up the next day? Materials I needed delivered early? Those kind of favors?" She pulled her hands from his. Her eyes narrowed. "You're Sally's "friend of a friend" person aren't you?" She tapped her foot. "I bet you arranged for my C.O. I'd wondered why the inspector didn't really look too hard."

"Abby, I'm sorry. I've been trying to figure out how to tell you." He dropped his gaze.

"So when you told me you understood, told me you thought I could handle the job—" She swallowed, the backs of her eyes burning with incipient tears. Her teeth clenched and she glared at him. "You lied."

His mouth moved as if to answer her, but no words emerged.

Looking down she saw her fingers entwine and break apart. The visual seemed like watching a nature program on worms, totally unrelated to her.

Moving her attention back to his face she said, "A short answer is all I need."

His answer came on a puff of air, a wisp that left her devastated. "Yes. I lied to you about calling in favors. I just wanted to help. But I do think you're competent. You didn't really need my assistance."

She turned her burning eyes back to watching her fingers twisting and turning. Her next words were spoken to her hands but meant for him.

"Why should I believe you now?" All the fatalism she held from a lifetime of disappointment resonated in the question.

She heard no ready answer. When she looked up, Carlos sat with his head bowed, his hands clasped between his knees. She left.

****

Carlos heard the outside door open and close. Every rustle and creak, the soft sound of the door shutting, sounded like the final voice of good-bye.

Mom had warned him but he hadn't listened. The worst part was that he had no excuse.

He'd wanted to stand next to her, to erase the sadness and give her someone she could count on to be on her side. All he'd accomplished? Adding more weight to the wrong side of the scale.

Henry stood, shook himself and walked over. He sat, his head against Carlos's knees.

"You're always here for me, aren't you? Can you teach me how to stop screwing up?"

The dog's head nudged his side.

He ran his hands over Henry's fur. The simple, familiar movement lifted some of his gloom.

He'd known he had to tell her what he'd done. Secrets never lasted long in Blue Peak. Definitely should have said something before they made love.

Damn. He'd been so stupid. He should return to counseling patients. Now he could empathize with bad life choices from personal experience.

Henry butted him. He resumed petting the dog. Henry had just reminded him that he'd gotten caught up in his plan and forgotten what was right. He'd lost track of why he wanted to help Abby. His ego had taken over.

Abby was right. She couldn't trust him.

A brisk knock sounded. Henry looked toward the door. Carlos's glance followed more slowly. Sally stuck her head into the room.

"Why are you sitting in here brooding? You've got customers out front."

Carlos remained sitting hunched over. "I'm not brooding."

"Hell, you could give a hen lessons. Want me to get you some eggs to warm?"

He glared at her, not answering.

"True love doesn't run smoothly. Believe me."

She held up her hand like a traffic policeman. "Now is not the time to discuss my failures. What are you doing about yours?"

"I'm so screwed."

"Self-pity won't help. You need a plan to get Abby back."

Carlos's laugh sounded sick, even to him. "A plan is what started this mess."

"I don't know about that but if I were you, I'd ban that bitch Jillian from the coffee house for life." She held up her hand. "I know I sound like a meanie. Jillian has problems, but she's old enough to control her emotions. Tossing her out on her ear would teach her a lesson she needs to learn. That'd be my first step in getting my woman back.

"Then I'd give Sierra the heave-ho. You don't need her okay to teach. Either the college wants you or they don't. She'd stick with you until the next better opportunity arose, then off she'd go, and I still wouldn't have grandchildren."

A faint smile decorated his lips. "Already figured that out, Mom."

"I'm glad my son has some common sense." She planted a fist on her hip. "After I had my house in order, I'd find Abby and keep talking until she listened to me."

She had a point. If nothing else, he'd take delight in denying Jillian access to one of her favorite pleasures. It's what she'd done to him.

"Now move your butt. If you act fast, I'll have a grandbaby by next spring. No woman wants to experience end-term pregnancy in August."

"Geez, Mom. Get me those eggs you mentioned. You have a better chance of me hatching a chick."

"Abby's the only chick that deserves your warmth and you know it. Now figure out a way to fix your mess. I want to see Abby smiling again, pronto."

Shit. He'd have more luck hatching unfertilized eggs.

Chapter Twenty-Four

I don't frickin' believe him. Is there a man in all of creation who doesn't lie?

Abby slammed the shovel into the pile of topsoil she'd had delivered, pushing with her work-booted foot. She threw her shovelful of dirt in the general direction of a wheelbarrow.

People all over town probably laughed behind her back thanks to Jillian.

Skanky. Her shovel bit into the ground.

Nauseating. Soil flew in every direction.

Devious. She loaded her shovel and more soil went flying.

Bitch, Jillian. The metal clanked against a rock. She tossed the tool down to the ground, her arms dangling. Her head drooped. Her lungs heaved.

Some dirt must have flown into her eyes; they felt gritty. It had to be that 'cause she wouldn't cry. The jerk didn't deserve her tears.

Her eyes clenched shut and she hugged herself until her knuckles turned white. Her body shook with the effort of controlling her emotions. Big girls don't cry. She remembered her mother's instructions too well. That didn't stop her tears.

"Are you okay?"

Carlos's hand touched her arm and dropped away. She turned her back on the familiar gesture. "What do you want? Haven't caused enough trouble so you came over to rustle up more?"

"Look, I'm sorry Jillian hurt you. I wanted to tell you what I'd done, but I couldn't figure out how."

She snorted. "A psych major that can't see the problem? Jillian's not the one who hurt me. Someone I considered a friend played that card."

"Friendship? Is that what you think we have? I have never known a woman like you." He ran his fingers through his hair. "I look at you and wonder what I could possibly have done to deserve a person like you. I know this may be too soon, but what we have is more than friendship to me."

She stood immobilized.

"Abby, we've made love. I need to see you and be with you on a regular basis. You're special to me."

"Sure, I'm special now. Another good-looking man like Rich—sweet talking me until a younger bit of fluff comes along. Or until you tire of me and return to your ex-fiancée. Well, I won't get caught again. I can't handle the pain."

"I'm not your ex, and I won't deliberately stomp on your heart. Didn't you hear what I said?" Carlos gasped for breath. "Do you know or have you any idea how hard this is for me to say? I thought you understood."

"This is all new for me. I've just moved in and there's so much work to do. Then Bunny came and now you, demanding. It's all too fast. I can't handle one more thing right now."

"So I'm a 'demanding thing.' Abby what I have to offer is more than a thing or a fling. Yes I know it's all happened fast, my brain is overloaded, too. But I think I can understand Sierra and why she acted as she did when she ran off. Sometimes love happens in a flash. All I ask is that you give me a chance, give *us* a chance before you refuse to see what we could have together."

Galvanized by the angry heat in Carlos's words, she blasted him back. She couldn't handle one more man telling her what to do with her life. "And all I ask is that you give me time. This is too much right now. I don't even know how I'll support myself or if my savings will last. I don't want to be needy. I have to know who I am. It's too much, Carlos, can't you see? I need more time. I want to make sure I do the right thing, make the best choice." Her voice broke.

"I understand, but don't wait too long, Abby. Life is short. I'll give you the space you need. If you want to see me again, you'll have to let me know. I won't come see you without an invitation."

****

Bunny sighed and looked at Abby from under her curly eyebrows.

"Don't you start with me."

The dog rose, huffed loudly, and moved to the lawn.

"Great, now my dog abandons me, too. I thought you were supposed to love me unconditionally," she called after Bunny.

Sally's convertible careened to a stop. She jumped out.

"Sweetie, don't let that bitch Jillian get between you and Carlos." She sat beside Abby giving her a one-armed hug. "Tell me how you're feeling, hon. Sorrow is easier to handle when the burden is shared."

Abby's jaw tightened. She scooted away. "You. You were in this together." She sniffed. "Poor little

Abigail. Can't handle a renovation alone. We'd better help her, son."

Sally covered her mouth with one hand. Tears stood in her eyes. "Is that what you think? Really? After accepting everyone's neighborly actions? You didn't understand, did you?"

Her stomach muscles cramped. "I did, I guess, but why? I mean, who am I to deserve that kind of attention?" She swallowed tears. "I trusted you. I thought you believed in me."

Sally shook her head. "You really don't know, do you?"

Abby wiped her cheeks with the back of her hand. "Know what."

"How beautiful you are. Oh, not just physically, but inside where it counts."

She hiccupped. "I don't understand."

"You've overcome a difficult life and are creating a beautiful home." Her neighbor handed her a wad of tissues. "I believe like attracts like. Many people want to make the world a better place, and when they see a person working on that, they join in. Happily. Because the project is something they can be proud of doing."

"Oh." Her chest muscles loosened.

"You know my stance on women. Do you really think I'd undermine you?"

She felt her face heat. "No, not really. I'm sorry."

"Apology accepted. Now, do you want to talk over anything with me?"

"I don't know where to start."

"How about where you feel comfortable."

"Okay." She hiccupped. "Gordon's story hit me in the gut because he had problems with his daughter, and

I never had a great relationship with my dad. He wasn't around often, and when he was, we didn't know how to talk together. I figured I wasn't good enough. And my mom, well I told you a little about her already."

"Parents can be total idiots. Me included."

She smiled. "Oh, I don't know. Carlos is okay." She frowned. "Well, he was until he lied."

"Back to you, sweetie. I think you have more to tell me."

"I guess." She balled the tissues in her fist. "Now I realize that I didn't know the whole story about my parents. About why they fought constantly. What I considered true could be a tale I created to deal with my own insecurities." She grabbed her friend's hand. "I don't know how to look at my girlhood feelings now that I'm older."

"There's no crime in fear. We all have some. You're facing your demons now, which is a task many people never take on. That takes courage. And for some, time."

She gulped and related her biggest dread. "I'm afraid I drove Carlos away. I just reacted, Sally. What does that say about me?"

"It says you're human. You have to heal your heart and invite him back. It's not an easy path you face, but I'm here to listen, if you want."

"I don't know. I'm not sure."

"We're here for you if you'll let us into your life. Carlos hurts, too. You can help each other heal. But first you have to decide what you want."

She nodded and hugged Sally tightly. "Thank you." She sniffled and wiped her nose.

"Call me, okay? I can see you need time to

yourself. You know where to find me." They hugged again.

"Thanks, again." She'd hang on to the lifeline Sally offered with everything she had in her.

****

Bunny stood at the front door barking. Abby pushed open the screen door and scanned the yard. Empty. Her dog ran down the steps and nosed at an object.

Great. Must be a dead something lying there. "Bunny, get away from that."

Bunny ignored her, swiping with her paw and sending the object sliding along the step.

"Oh, for goodness' sake. What do you have there?" She moved to the bottom stair, gently moving her dog aside. The sun broke through, its rays warming the back of her neck as she stared at a small package.

"Oh." Lydia's wooden box, wrapped in clear plastic, rested before her.

Once again, she scanned the yard. Still empty of people, though birds chirped and sung. Bunny barked once, short and sharp.

Hands shaking, she picked up the wrapped box, turned and entered the house with the dog leading. She continued through the rooms and out to the patio, sinking onto her lawn chair. The box slipped off her lap when the dog jumped up beside her.

"Gordon? The box is unlocked. I know you told me to read the letters, but I'll give you one last chance to change your mind."

A warm breeze picked up. His soft response sounded in her ear. "Read them."

She took a deep breath and flipped the lid open.

Two letters of disparate sizes were inside. The flaps' gum was long gone; the envelopes open to time. On the front of each was written, "Julia" in beautiful penmanship with faded but still legible ink. The smaller envelope held a notation written with darker ink saying, "open this first."

Her unsteady hands and trembling fingers fumbled with the envelope's flap, eventually withdrawing a sheaf of plain stationary.

Dearest Julia,

I wrote the enclosed letter shortly after your birth. I hoped to share the information when you turned twenty-one. You know better than I what caused you to leave home after high school. Please believe I hoped for a reunion because I missed you every day. You will find this after I am dead and I apologize for not telling you face-to-face. I'm sorry I wasn't a better mother. Please know that I love you with all my heart.

Forgive me,

Mom

Abby's heart pounded. These letters weren't meant for her. She shouldn't read the one waiting within the box. This wasn't her business.

"I want you to read the second letter," Gordon said. "You deserve to know the truth. Someone needs to know, in case Julia rejects the package." He paused. "Besides, you've helped me."

She sat quietly, taking deep breaths to slow her pulse. Other families experienced trouble besides hers. Daughters walked away, parents grieved. Plenty of books and movies sang the same song. So why did she feel reluctant about opening this second letter?

Abby rubbed her forehead. She'd been running for too long, and Gordon's tone suggested reading Julia's letter could help her. She blew a breath and grasped the letter, opening it with deference to its fragility.

Dearest Julia,

I write this letter as you lie in your bassinet, new to this world and to our family. So small, so precious, and so adored.

I plan to tell you this story in person when you're older but life is unpredictable. This letter may take my place. If you're like me you're probably wondering what this is about and why I don't cut to the chase.

Your Daddy, the man who watches over and cares for you, is not your birth father.

You'll learn that your Daddy can be a difficult man but he means well. But never think that he did not want you. He couldn't wait to see you born. His hands trembled when he held you for the first time. I hope that your memories of him, of us, are of good times together.

Your birth father wasn't in my life for long. The reasons I went with this other man are not important, and he left town long before you were born. He never knew about you, and I didn't know how to contact him. I like to believe he was an angel come to Earth just to give me you.

If I were you right now, I'd be very angry with my parents. That's why I hope that you'll remember how much we loved you. Because in this moment as I watch you sleep, I can only envision many years of happiness together.

We cannot know what the years will bring us. I hope you will always know love.

Love,

Your Mother

Abby carefully refolded the letter and slid it back into the envelope. She replaced both letters in the box, laid the lock on top of the letters and closed the lid.

Gordon's telling her about Lydia's affair still hadn't prepared her. Not for the swelling emotion overtaking her.

Wow.

Just, wow.

Chapter Twenty-Five

Abby's kitchen floor design was almost complete. She'd worked non-stop since reading the letters, with breaks only to feed Bunny or let her in and out of the house. She vaguely remembered eating a sandwich.

Bunny had lain in the doorway watching her and acting as a sounding board. The little dog had earned Abby's trust and love simply by remaining at her side.

The painting consumed her, but at some point during the night, her hands began operating independently of her mind. There, in the dark, still hours after midnight, she'd delved into her past and taken a long look at her life. Yes, her dread of opening herself to others loomed large over the years. She saw how she'd hidden behind fear to avoid being hurt.

Her stubborn streak kept her painting long after her muscles rebelled. She felt like a piece of balsa wood in a high wind. Emotionally and physically limp, she was mentally clear for the first time, probably ever. She had fears; she didn't need to let her fears own her.

She stretched. When a tobacco smell surrounded her, she blinked at the clock then out the windows. Sunrise. Her knees and back ached.

"Will you stop for a while?" Gordon sounded gruff. "Or do you plan to hide out in perpetuity?"

"I'm not hiding. Besides, I'm surprised you're still here. Weren't you leaving after the letters were found? I

213

promise to send them on later today."

"Puppy. I can see what's what. Don't be a ninny. You're making the same mistake I made, first with Lydia then Julia."

"What do you mean?"

"You use your work to escape. That's why you're always busy. You think I don't recognize the symptoms?"

"I think that was true before, now the work has helped me put my life into perspective."

"How's that?"

"Did you know that the rose is an ancient symbol of love and beauty? The Greeks and Romans considered the rose a symbol of their Goddesses of Love, Aphrodite and Venus. Gordon, Delia told me that Lydia was known for her roses."

"That's true. Those gardener friends of hers were always after her hybrids. She spent a lot of time in her garden."

"Did it never occur to you that Lydia's garden was an expression of her eternal love for you? You both worked so hard to prove your love to each other you forgot to receive."

She didn't hear his response. "Gordon?"

"I'm here."

"I've been running from life because I couldn't accept my experiences or myself as I am. You helped me see that life means taking chances and forgiving mistakes. My mistakes and those the people around me made."

"Hmph. Well, good."

"I'll continue making mistakes. I guess that's how I learn."

"That's because you're a puppy."

Laughter swelled her chest. She wished she'd known him when he was alive. Her thoughts sobered. "Gordon, this painted floor is my thanks to you and to Lydia. It's not done yet, and it may be covered by a future owner, but my love and gratitude for you will always be here."

When he didn't answer, she continued, assuming he was embarrassed with her words.

"I promise to send the box and letters on to Julia."

"And?"

"And I understand. I understand why I've lived the way I have. My life unfolded according to my choices."

"Good. I take it you plan to change?"

"Yes. How about you? Have you come to grips with the mistakes you made and will you forgive yourself?"

Silence ensued, then Gordon said, "You're a pretty smart puppy for a girl who doesn't know much. Julia may not forgive Lydia or me, but I did my best. That's all anyone can do."

She heard his muffled voice say, "Lydia, is that you?"

"Gordon?"

"Thanks for everything, Abby. See you later."

"Gordon?" She received no answer.

The door to the patio opened without visible means and outside the rose bushes rustled in calm morning air. Bunny raised her muzzle from off her paws and tilted her head. She watched the patio intently.

Gordon faced his wife. "Lydia. You've come back for me."

"I've been here all along waiting for you to see me.

You always were a stubborn old coot."

"You mean I didn't have to wait here in limbo until she found your letters?"

Lydia shook her head. "No, you could have left and had another chance to fix things with Julia at a different time. You chose to help Abby. That's why you didn't see me at your side."

"She'll be okay, won't she?"

"Abby will be just fine. I love what she's done with the house."

"I thought you would. She'll get the box and letters to Julia."

"I heard. You did well, Gordon. It's time to go." Lydia smiled and held out her hand to him.

He grasped it, at ease now with change. "Do you think we'll be able to come back to check on the house?"

"I think that can be arranged." She tugged his hand. "Come." They moved toward a growing focus of light, disappearing into its center.

The rose bushes stopped rustling and the patio door closed gently. Bunny placed her muzzle back onto her paws and closed her eyes. Abby sensed the house shift around her. She knew Gordon had finally moved on.

Abby slid to the floor and rested her back against the wall. Her thoughts, which should be chattering, instead focused on one idea. Being alone didn't scare her. She didn't feel lonely, knowing she now had her home to herself. Sure, she'd miss Gordon's corny jokes and even his pipe tobacco scent, but his moving on seemed right, timely. She was glad she'd been part of his growth, knowing he'd been essential to hers.

She stretched her sore muscles and went to shower.

The floor hadn't been completed but at least she'd given him a gift before he left. She smiled as she realized one of her dreams would come true because of a ghost. Wait until she told Sally.

****

Abby folded the bottom of the priority-mailing box closed, taping it tightly. She tried to imagine Julia's reaction when the box Gordon had said he'd fashioned by hand for Lydia arrived. Happy? Angry? Sorry she ran away?

Then she wondered what she'd do if two letters from the past arrived out of nowhere. Not that anything similar would happen to her. Although she'd wanted different parents when she heard their bitter fights. Maybe lots of kids felt that way, especially after they were disciplined, or if they had a home filled with anger.

She placed a short hand-written note to the attorney with Lydia's box, wrapping them both in protective material. A little voice asked her, *and what about you? Aren't you ready for some happiness?*

A sense of entitlement begged for attention. As she examined the idea a feeling of lightness enveloped her. Yes, she did deserve to have her dreams come true.

She slipped Julia's packet into the shipping box and sealed it. Whistling cheerfully she found the address of the attorney that had acted for Julia in the house sale.

"Okay, Gordon, the package is ready to go."

Now it was time for her to keep a promise to herself. She counted herself damn lucky Carlos was a patient man.

****

217

Carlos sat at his desk, irritated with everyone. He pulled a stack of invoices closer. After the initial movement they remained unnoticed and untouched. He mulled his recent decisions.

He'd spoken with the college and made an appointment with the dean for later that week. Abby's suggestion to teach part-time had been a good one, because he'd discovered he didn't want to give up the Collective Unconscious Café. Carlos hoped he'd work something out with the college, but decided he could be happy with the status quo.

Sierra had arrived at the coffee house not long after his call to the dean's office. Her smile had dimmed when he told her that not only had nothing been settled, his possible return to teaching didn't mean they'd pick up their relationship. He had no delusions about her pining for him, or that his love belonged to another woman.

He hadn't seen Jillian since banning her from his café. Guess she finally got the message. Thank God. He'd never been closer to a charge of Murder One. Or felt such a sense of satisfaction at seeing her face pale upon hearing him eighty-six her from the coffee house. He hadn't decided if her blanched appearance was caused by anger or another emotion. He didn't give a damn.

None of his actions made him miss Abby less. His attention wandered until he saw nothing, not even Henry sprawled on his dog bed. When his phone sounded, he let it ring multiple times before jerking the receiver up with a curse.

"Yes."

"Carlos. It's Abby."

His breath caught. He pounded his fist against his chest twice before answering. "Hi."

"Thank you for leaving the unlocked box, but you could have knocked on the door."

What could he say? Seeing that box on his desk had torn his heart to pieces. He'd dropped it off to get it out of his sight. "I'd promised to get it opened. And I didn't think you wanted to see me."

"Yeah, well, you were right. And now you're wrong."

His pulse leaped. "What do you mean?"

"Gordon helped me to see that life can't be controlled. Plus, I've been carrying around hurt for years. Some people aren't always meant to be together. Rich and I, well, he's better off with a woman who loves him totally. And dealing with my fears is necessary."

Did she mean her words? Had she really worked out her stuff? Sure, she was strong, but she'd been so unsure and angry yesterday. This better not be a game. He was sick to damn death of games.

"I don't know, Abby. Your words sound good, but how can I trust what you're saying?"

He listened to silence. Damn it. He'd screwed up again.

"You're right, I guess. I've kept you at a distance and run before you could explain yourself. I understand you'd be leery."

He wanted to see her expressions. Inhale her scent. They shouldn't have this conversation over the phone.

"Don't move. Not a muscle. I'll be right over."

Carlos didn't bother attaching Henry's leash. They jumped into the car and left, breaking traffic laws along the way. He parked and slid out, leaving his car door open. Henry ran before him, barking.

"Abby!" He knocked on the door. "Damn it. Where are you?"

"Kitchen."

He threw open the door and raced in after his dog. Abby stood next to the cabinet, her phone in her hand.

"You told me not to move a muscle. Did you know you can't end a call without muscles?"

He ran his hands through his hair. "I don't believe you're so literal."

"I'm not, or I wouldn't be speaking. That takes muscles, too." She put her phone down. "I think I'm in shock that you arrived so soon."

He enfolded her in his arms. "Did you mean what you said on the phone? I don't want to lose you again."

"I've done a lot of thinking. Maybe too much thinking. All I know for sure is that we don't know what will happen or if a lasting love will develop between us. But I want to give whatever we have a try, if you'll still have me. My work… you know I'm not finished healing."

Carlos bent his head. "I can't think of anyone I'd rather learn with." He kissed her. "And to paraphrase a smart woman I know, emotional work, like a house, may never be done."

He straightened. "Along those lines, I need your input."

"Would you like a seat on the couch to discuss your problems, Herr Young?"

"Not a problem, just, well, I've never known my father. I think it's time to discover more about him. Do you think I'll hurt Mom by investigating?"

"I think you'll be doing her a favor. If I've read her inferences correctly, letting him go was a mistake she's regretted for years." She smoothed his shirtfront. "Besides, I'd like nothing better than giving Sally some of her own back."

"Bloodthirsty wench, aren't you?"

"You have no idea."

Chapter Twenty-Six

"Is there a reason you have to do everything yourself?" Carlos gritted his teeth. "The party isn't until tomorrow night, Abby. I'm here to help you, remember?"

"What?" Abby blinked.

Carlos took a deep breath. "Any reason you're not letting me assist you?"

Abby frowned. "I thought I was."

"Uh, huh. That's why I have to fight you to lift the heavy stuff and push you aside to get at the boxes you want moved."

"Well—"

"Well what?" Carlos felt his control slip. Did he have to spell everything out for this woman?

"I guess I'm accustomed to working alone. Pulling my weight."

"No, I'd say you're a control freak who can't trust anyone to handle things as well as you can."

She crossed her arms. "No, I don't think so, not anymore."

He copied her body language. "Really? So that's why you followed me when I carried your grandmother's mirror this morning, rubbing your hands together every time I took a step."

"Uh, I did?" Her arms loosened their grip around her torso.

He nodded. "Yep, and then you hopped from foot-to-foot when I hung it for you."

"Oh."

"Oh," he echoed. He tilted his head as he slapped his palms against his hips. "I'm starting to wonder if you need me around."

"I do."

He blew a sigh. "You have a strange way of showing your need." He walked to the door.

"Carlos." He halted.

She hurried over to him, placing her hand tentatively on his shoulder. "I'm sorry. I just don't know what you want. You're not like—"

"Not like?" He turned toward her, his right eyebrow raised.

"Well, I've never had a man want to help me before."

His left eyebrow met his right above his nose. "Why not? I'd like to help you all day."

"Most of the guys I've known, well, I guess I was the one to take care of them." She rubbed her arms. "Although I've recognized that maybe I didn't give anyone a chance to offer."

His voice soft he said, "So don't you think it's time someone cared for you?" Carlos lightly touched her jaw with his fingers. "Abby. Let me help you."

Taking a deep breath she said, "You'll be sorry you offered."

"And why is that?"

"I'm a taskmaster. I'll have you jumping. And you'd better do a good job."

"Ooh, a dominatrix in disguise as a cheerleader. I'll do my very best to satisfy you."

"I'm talking about the work around here. My to-do list is full. There's a lot to accomplish before the party."

His eyes darkened, a spark lit his pupils. "All I can think about right now is the item that's at the top of my own list."

She backed away from him. "Somehow I think our lists may not be synchronized."

He followed her. His tongue ran over the top of her ear. "Are you sure our lists aren't in synch?"

Her neck swayed to the side, and her body relaxed. She twined her arms around his neck and rubbed her breasts against his chest. Then she licked and nipped her way across his jaw toward his ear.

Carlos smiled. Her actions excited his body while tentacles of calm wrapped around his heart. He was one lucky dog.

****

Abby stretched languidly, the early afternoon sun peeking through her bedroom window. The tentative rays highlighted the dusty brown sprinkling of hair on Carlos's bare leg resting heavily over hers.

She turned her head. He slept easily, a slight smile on his face. Her fingers itched to massage his chest. After all, turnabout was fair play. She nestled closer.

This man knew how to push her buttons. All her hard-won focus had been blown. The thought didn't bother her as much as it once would have. Her fingers moved all on their own down his chest toward his hips. He moaned, his penis twitched toward wakefulness.

Well, if her schedule had been ruined, she'd just have to make Carlos work a little harder. She giggled and applied herself to reordering her priorities. They'd better hurry. They still had work to do outside.

****

Sally bustled into Abby's backyard. "Hi, cutie."

Abby reached for her friend. "Sally!"

"Hi, Carlos. Fancy seeing you here."

His lips quirked. "Mom."

"We brought you annuals. You could use some color back here. Can't have a party tomorrow without flowers."

"Oh, but—"

"No, buts. This won't take long."

Sally called to her friends as she walked around the corner. Abby smiled. Just a few weeks ago, she would've been trying to figure out how to pay her back for the flowers. Now she knew that these gestures were normal between friends and neighbors. Life was a circle of gratitude not quid pro quo.

Her voluntary gardeners argued good naturedly as they walked into the yard toting flats of colorful blooms. She roused herself and headed back into the house. Her reordered priorities had left her with a ton of work inside, and the garden was under control.

Hands covered her eyes later that afternoon. Abby shivered. She knew those hands. A low voice whispered into her ear. "I've got a surprise for you." She knew that voice, too.

"Keep your eyes closed."

"Why—"

"Just keep them closed."

She heard a whisper of soft material then felt it slide across her cheekbones. It smelled like Carlos. Her bones softened like warm rubber.

Her abductor adjusted the silken mask over her eyes, secured it. His muscular arms tightened around her, pulling her back against his chest. "You're my prisoner. Don't try to escape or your punishment will go hard on you." His wet, hot mouth attacked the nape of her neck. His erection pressed against her buttocks.

"Don't forget for one moment that I'm in control."

Her body sagged against him. "Is that a threat or a promise?"

A low chuckle filled her ear. "You decide."

Her body grew taut. *What kind of surprise waited?*

He stepped away, hands firm on her upper arms, spinning her before directing her out of the room.

Senses alert, listening for the slightest sound, Abby's disorientation increased her pulse rate and respiration. She stumbled, his arms supporting and righting her, drawing her onward. A door creaked open, fresh air teased her nostrils. Outside. But at the front or back of the house? Back. No street noise and the scent of fresh mulch filled the air.

"Where are we going?"

"No questions."

"But—"

"You'll see soon enough."

Her sensitized skin felt his hands moving up her arm, slowly, aiming to tantalize. She shivered again, unable to control the sensations running through her. If he gave regular lessons on relinquishing control, she might be tempted to attend class. His lips lit on the silk above each eye in turn then addressed her forehead. Her chin came up, lips pursed, inviting his mouth to settle on hers.

Carlos ignored the invitation. "Are you ready for your surprise?"

Abby nodded. The silk rustled and slid down her

face, releasing a flood of sensuality. She opened her eyes.

Before her stood the scene she'd visualized days ago—a small iron table with chairs, a carafe of coffee, mugs, the drone of bees, a small vase of roses. Only the book was missing. Her mouth dropped open. "How did you know?"

"I saw it at the used furniture store and thought of you."

"They told you I wanted the patio set, didn't they?"

"I suppose I'll have to tell the truth, even though I wanted you to think I found it on my own."

She took a hop, jumping straight up to land in his arms, her legs wrapped around his waist. "You are amazing. So is this town."

His expression turned dark. Settling herself in his arms, she leaned back, yanking open her shirt. "Like what you see, big boy?"

His thumbs caressed her buttocks, his hands spread out in support. "Perhaps I should inspect the goods?"

"Be my guest. Wouldn't want you disappointed later on. I don't give refunds."

His tongue caressed her nipple. "I've heard turnabout is fair play," he mumbled around his mouthful. He turned his attention to her other breast.

"You know, I've heard the same thing."

Heat shot from her breasts to her core. His fingers squeezed and caressed her bottom even as his erection strained toward the juncture of her thighs. She panted. "I think we should move inside. Get rid of these clothes."

He grunted. What did that mean? His open-mouthed kisses stopped, a cool breeze wafting over her chest replaced his heat. He loosened his grip. She dropped to her feet, sliding down his front all the way. Oh, he'd grunted in agreement.

Abby saw the silk and pulled the necktie from his slack grip. She balanced it on her finger. "Maybe it's your turn to be blindfolded."

"Is that a threat or a promise?" His answering grin had her expecting sharp incisors erupting from his gums.

"You decide. Meanwhile, you've got work in my bedroom. I've just added a new item to my list."

Chapter Twenty-Seven

Carlos and Abby were setting up the drinks table for her party that night. She threw her arms around him, planting a kiss just below his ear. She whispered, "Have I told you how much I appreciate your help?"

He smiled. "Every day in all kinds of ways. It's my pleasure." He felt her hands wringing together at the back of his neck. "Stop worrying. The house looks great."

"Are you sure? Everyone will know it's not finished completely, right?"

Carlos wrapped his arms around her. "Your house looks spectacular and yes, everyone will understand. So can I help you work out your pre-party jitters? I've got some ideas that may fit the bill."

His voice rumbled in her mid-section. He laid a string of kisses from her ear down her jaw.

Bunny and Henry dashed into the room, tumbling to a stop against Carlos's legs.

"Oof. What's this?" He laughed. "Looks like our dogs are hungry. Did we forget to feed them?"

She answered without pause, "They've been fed, the little beggars." Then it hit her. He'd referred to "our dogs." She examined that concept and decided it sounded just right.

****

The house shone with lamplight and the glow of

229

people enjoying each other. "That Old Black Magic" played quietly in the background.

"Abby, your party's a hit." Sally hugged her. "Your guests can't stop talking about your breakfast nook and floor. So when will you start advertising?"

Abby's bright face eclipsed a Las Vegas casino's for wattage. "Carlos commissioned me for Collective Unconscious. And one of the Garden Club ladies wants me to call her. My career dream could come true, right?"

"I have no doubts. And neither should you."

"Well, then, would you help me set up a company?"

"I'd like nothing better."

Delia approached them, her copper bracelet shimmering at her wrist. "Abby, dear, my husband has a question for you."

As they left, Carlos joined Sally. "All Abby's talked about tonight is how the house will look when it's done instead of apologizing like crazy for not being finished, yet." He tilted his head. "You've really helped her."

Sally patted his hand. "We all worked together. You, me, Blue Peak folks, and most of all, Abby herself." She hugged him and moved off.

Carlos surveyed the room taking in the movement of people who formed and reformed like a kaleidoscope. The noise level had elevated and everyone looked at ease. He wasn't surprised that she'd organized her house and the party in just a week. She continually amazed him.

He moved to Abby. Drawing her back against his chest he breathed into her ear, "You're a hit."

Abby nestled against him. "Thanks for helping me get ready this week. I enjoyed having you around. I never knew a to-do list should be a guide, not a priority until you. Thanks."

"Did you enjoy me enough that I can come over even though the work's done?"

She looked over her shoulder. "Didn't you know? A house is never finished." She turned and smoothed his fish-shaped tie. "Neither are we."

****

Gordon and Lydia sat at the table on the patio, watching former friends and neighbors enjoy their old home.

"Delia saved the roses. Thank you for getting her over here." Lydia patted his hand.

"Hmph. I couldn't let that puppy, ah, Abby, ruin them, could I? You'd have held me responsible for eternity."

"I noticed she framed our photograph for her mantel," Lydia said.

"Yep. Surprised me."

"Oh, Gordon, not really. You acted like a father toward her, and she forwarded those letters to Julia. She responded like a family member. For you."

"I guess."

Lydia chuckled. "You never did want compliments."

"About those letters…I heard Abby tell the little hippie girl that Julia's lawyer called. He has confirmation that she's received your letters. Do you think she's read them, yet?"

Her phantom hand clasped his. "Dear, you did your part. We can't control the reactions of others, especially those we love. I have faith she'll find her way."

"So you're saying we won't ever know the outcome?"

"No, I'm saying we can check in with her." She shook her finger in his face. "No tobacco scent tricks or blasting Julia with cold air. Look, don't touch."

"You really were watching over me, weren't you?"

"As if you ever doubted I would."

They tapped ghostly feet to the music.

"Listen, Doris Day."

"One of my favorites, 'Que Sera, Sera.'"

"I can take credit for that," Gordon said. "I encouraged her to develop a good taste in music."

"Gordon, it's our last visit here. We're going to be busy with after-life lessons and other duties." She savored the yard illuminated with a party glow.

He coughed into his hand. "It'll be good to get back to work."

Her emotions shimmered in her aura. She held out pale arms. "Dance with me?"

"Do I have to?"

"Please?"

"I'm still being an ass, I suppose."

"I shouldn't say."

"You never did set me straight often enough." He stood and bowed from the waist. "My dear, my only love, will you dance with me?"

"Yes, to my everlasting pleasure."

The spectral couple came together, found the beat and twirled, waltzing to the music. The music ended, the breeze around them stilled. Then the air swirled and popped as their forms dissolved. Bright dots of color flashed like a swarm of multi-colored lightning bugs rising for the tree tops.

A whirlwind scattered the colors. When the breeze died, a pipe slowly revolved in the center of the table.

A word about the author...

Ashantay Peters loves escaping into a well-written book. She lives in the mountains of western North Carolina, a happy transplant from the much colder (and flatter) Midwest.

Besides communing with ghosts, Ashantay enjoys writing murder mysteries. Well, the two do kind of go together.

Please contact the author through the following links. She promises not to stalk you.

www.ashantay.com
ashantay.peters@gmail.com
~*~

Other Ashantay Peters titles
available from The Wild Rose Press, Inc.:
DEATH STRETCH
DEATH UNDER THE MISTLETOE
DEATH RUB
DICKENS OF A DEATH

Thank you for purchasing
this publication of The Wild Rose Press, Inc.

If you enjoyed the story, we would appreciate your
letting others know by leaving a review.

For other wonderful stories,
please visit our on-line bookstore at
www.thewildrosepress.com.

For questions or more information
contact us at
info@thewildrosepress.com.

The Wild Rose Press, Inc.
www.thewildrosepress.com

Stay current with The Wild Rose Press, Inc.

Like us on Facebook

https://www.facebook.com/TheWildRosePress

And Follow us on Twitter
https://twitter.com/WildRosePress

www.ingramcontent.com/pod-product-compliance
Lightning Source LLC
Chambersburg PA
CBHW070920180626
46817CB00003B/1141